MOONLIGHT REBORN

MIYO HUNTER

1

SOFIA

I wasn't the type that the moon should choose.

Not now, when the population was down, and fewer wolves emerged among the people each year. But when the moonlight whispered, it woke something within me. Something that had been sleeping, deep within my blood. Though I always knew that I carried the bloodline, it was never supposed to be me...

Growing up, adults would smile if I brought up that I could be a wolf. But it was the kind of strained indulgent smile that didn't truly believe. Didn't quite reach the eyes. No one ever admitted to my face that it was because I was too weak. Scrawny. For most of my youth, I was all awkward elbows and knobby knees. I was never climbing the highest trees or mastering combat skills. That was always my sister.

It was supposed to be her.

It was no wonder that my father agreed to let me go for the trade—an exchange of the firstborn children of the alphas.

I could still feel the soft wrinkles of my grandmother's

fingers as she held my face in her hands and said, "What you are doing is brave. You are saving our tribe from war."

Holding on to those soft wrinkled palms was like holding on to her kind words, and somehow to the rest of my family as well. But I had been forced to let her go. I had to.

As the firstborn of the Edgeriver tribe, I showed no weakness as I crossed the line over enemy territory. I held my eyes wide open to keep them dry. I was sent to live here, among my enemies, told that they would treat me like their own daughter. That the exchange would ensure that no further blood would be shed. Neither side would have to lose any more wolves.

As I crossed the line over to the enemy territory, I couldn't help but look at the firstborn child who would take my place, and my home. Sandy-haired and thin, he walked with his head high and didn't return my gaze. He crossed wide meadows to the row of pine trees that marked the edge of the territory and fell out of view before he got to my mother and father.

I was supposed to be treated like family, but I knew my place. I knew what I really was—a hostage. Both of us children were. A threat to hold over my people. All to stop the decades-long feud that had lost too many of the bloodline in a never-ending cycle.

The moment I was in reach, the alpha grabbed my chin, pressing upward to force my gaze to meet his.

Those born into my tribe had eyes the color of the rich warmth of the soil. The brown of mother earth from which everything grows. My eyes were the pale color of storm clouds and trouble on the horizon. The natural hue washed away, leaving me with a gaze piercing as ice. Cold.

Was it a sign that I was always meant to be an outsider?

Always meant to be traded away? I forced myself to maintain eye contact, though I wanted to look away before he noticed the strange color and thought he'd been tricked.

"This is what they send me in exchange for my eldest?" The alpha's nostrils flared wide.

I swallowed down my protests, well aware that they could see my small frame. I was no warrior.

"Take her to the kitchens and make sure she eats something. Don't want blood on my hands because the water child keeled over on my watch."

Dismissed already.

A rough arm took hold of my shoulder and pulled me away.

Weak. Forgotten. Not strong enough to continue the bloodline, nor to carry the spirit of the wolf.

That was how I had been chosen to end the bloodshed.

Five Years Later

The night of the vernal equinox was a full moon. As the sky darkened, two weeks after my eighteenth birthday, I was led to the old growth forest with all my peers who recently turned of age.

I stayed away from the others, halfway in the shadows. They raised their heads to the sky, welcoming the pale rays of the moon on their skin, as I watched half-terrified that as soon as one of them shifted they would scent me out as the enemy.

Dried ink on the treaty wouldn't stop fresh blood from spilling on the ground, not for any new-turned wolf. I could always tell who held the spirit of the wolf—the ones looking at me like I would make a particularly delicious meal. I could see it in their eyes, hear warnings growled out if I got too close. There was no way a wolf shifting for the first time would see me as anything other than the enemy.

The moment moonlight touched my skin, it bloomed—the energy heated through my veins. It itched and scratched at my bones, howling within me. My body was a cage too fragile to contain the beast that was thrashing against my ribs, fighting to break free.

I held in my gasp so as to not alert the others. I took a few shaky steps back, as quietly as I could, until I could slink deeper into the old foliage. I got away. The others should have noticed me slinking out of sight, but they were used to ignoring me.

The pressure started in my mouth—my jaw elongated, as teeth grew into fangs piercing the gums, and the skin of my face split apart with the strain. My thumbs cracked, breaking away from my palms, as the bone slid upward. Skin tore as claws burst through my fingertips. My bones twisted, cracking in places, as I was reformed. Pain I could handle, but more than the pain, I felt something stirring in my mind, shaking off years of sleep. A presence that was older than my eighteen years. Old as the forest.

I took a deep breath, taking in everything—I could smell time. In the air. In the urine and sweat marking the movements of all the creatures around. One deep breath told me the diet of the rabbits in the area. Which of the deer were aging. I could scent out the trails of all that lived in these woods. None as strong as me.

The beast within me licked her chops. She was hungry.

I ran through the forest, exhilarated. Other senses stirred awake, clawing at me from the back of my mind.

The smells of the forest were overwhelming. Rancid smells, moist smells. The smells of droppings, the smells of flowers and dew. All of it was mixed together in a mush that didn't make sense. It felt like static, all coming at once.

I could smell people. Their scents were like neon signs in my mind. I choose my paths as far away from them as I dared.

I raced through the forest; my feet—no, my paws—ate up the ground. I didn't know where I was going until I reached the edge of the river.

The human within me froze, forcing the wolf back.

What the hell was I doing?

I was face-to-face with the edge of the territory, staring right at my homeland. The land I grew up in. The land that wasn't my home anymore. If I made another move, as soon as I crossed the river, it would be a violation of the treaty. War would start back up again. People would die, and it would be all my fault.

The wolf whimpered, scenting home.

My pack.

Their fur and their urine marked the trees just on the other side. Lights in the distance marked where my father sat inside, smoking his pipe. Where my sister curled up in front of the hearth to read.

I can't. It's not my home anymore.

Why did I get the blessing of the moon on enemy land? Far from where the strength of the wolf could help my people.

As I forced myself to return, the grip of the moon slipped away. I dropped to the ground as my bones shrunk and skin erupted back over my form. My skin felt raw. My whole body shook, swaying as I forced myself upright.

I was naked, and alone.

Maybe I should signal for help? I had made it close enough back to the castle that wolves on patrol would be able to find me. A new wolf was cause for celebration. But I couldn't shake the feeling that I would be shunned for it. I was ostensibly now one of the daughters of the alpha. Practically royalty. None of the Stonevalley wolves treated me that way. They couldn't control their reflex to wrinkle their noses at me, as if they smelled something foul.

I am not pack here.

What was I going to do?

My wolf was new and fierce and didn't deserve to be forced to the bottom of the social hierarchy, to be harassed by the others.

The best thing that I could hope to do would be to hold back and hide it. It wasn't as if anyone could look at me and tell that something was wrong. That there was a beast that ripped through me, changing everything.

For now, I would just remain hidden.

My bare feet walked cautiously. I winced as the newly formed skin trod on rocks and sharp branches. But I wouldn't give up. I wouldn't call attention to myself.

I approached one of the drop offs: storage containers with spare clothes for any wolves caught out without clothes after shifting.

I paused behind the bushes, listening. If I listened hard enough, I could hear people talking, but it seemed to be at a distance that was too far for human ears. As I focused, my vision dulled. Colors like red and purple dimmed into grays and blacks. It was disorienting.

I only caught snatches of conversations, though the wolf in me could tell that they were miles away.

"Didn't hear any howling or anything."

"Fewer of us every year."

There didn't seem to be anyone near the drop off for miles. I approached the storage box and pulled off the plastic lid. Inside, there was clothing of all shapes. I grabbed the smallest pair of jeans, a white shirt that fit like a tent, and shoes that pinched.

Clutching the bark of the tree, at the edge of the forest, I listened, straining my senses. The night was quieting down. I didn't scent any of my peers making the change in the clearing around me, and I had kept quiet about my own transformation. With any luck, my absence had been missed.

The castle walls were empty. Now in the dead of the night, they looked practically barren.

Perfect. There wasn't anyone around. I crossed the field to the castle as quickly as I dared. Quick movements would draw the eyes of a predator. But I was in no mood to linger about, waiting to get caught.

I chanced going in through a back doorway. Not that I had any keys on me. It was a shabby entrance for deliveries and frequently I found it to be unlocked.

If this didn't work, I might have to go through the grand front gates. Even this late, there was sure to be members of the pack awake. Holding out a hope that some of the young awakened under the force of the moon to join their ranks in the pack.

Before the wolves viewed me poorly enough when I was just a human. Now when I was an enemy wolf, what would they do to me?

I got to the door, pushing it open with relief. I got in, unnoticed.

For now, my secret was safe.

Fatigue hit me all at once. It felt like taking off a well-worn jacket and then having all the cool air hit. Tonight was a lot to handle, and it wasn't just the change. I hadn't ventured so close to my home, not since I was first taken away from there, and that was years ago.

"What the fuck are *you* doing here?"

I gasped. I knew that deep voice, aimed at me in practically a snarl.

What the hell was *he* doing here?

Aaron Ragnolf.

His hair was the color of dried out grass, with intense blue eyes flashing in anger. Broad and well-muscled enough to seem like a threat, even with the strength of the wolf lying within me, ready to rise to the surface.

According to the laws of the trade, he was technically my family now. I was meant to be a member of the royal family, welcomed in with open arms.

Aaron didn't see me that way. Quick to send a glare or a cutting comment to let me know that I was not wanted.

He was the last person I wanted to see tonight, or any night. I couldn't let him get a good look, not now. Not with my skin raw and drenched in the scent of the forest. He'd always looked too close, been a little too interested in my affairs. He had always sniffed around me like I was about to commit some kind of crime. Like it was *my* fault that his precious older brother was taken away, and that I should personally be held accountable for it.

I ducked my head down and quickened my pace, hoping to slip past him.

"Hey, you better answer when I'm talking to you."

Aaron grabbed my forearm, grasping me in a bruising grip that bit deep, all the way into my newly reformed tendons and muscles.

But as soon as his skin touched mine, electricity sparked. An ancient power burned white-hot across my forearm. For the second time that night, my body reacted as something lying dormant within me clawed its way to the surface. It was a force of nature. Within me, my wolf pressed her nose upward to the full-bright power of the moon and howled.

Across my forearm the mark was unmistakable, in an angry raised brand. It could only mean one thing. *It could not possibly mean... It couldn't be.*

The second son of the Stonevalley tribe, and heir to the alpha, was my soulmate.

My nose flared as I took in the scent of her. Ripe, with traces of forest and soil, and dusky floral undertones. Sofia Decoteau—no, Ragnolf. She was a Ragnolf now. A member of my own family.

She is not *my sister.*

I ripped my hands off her, staring at the mark branded into my palm where I had touched her. I had thought that I had found her sneaking out. Possibly to meet a disreputable male, or to trade in secrets about my family.

But this was something else.

She could not possibly be a wolf. The sentinels declared this entire group of our young yielded nothing.

But the mark burned into my flesh said otherwise. Only a fellow wolf could trigger this.

She was out late because she had turned. Though she was trying to hide it, Sofia was a wolf.

I stared at the brand on my skin, unable to rip my eyes away from it. From the angry raised swirls that twisted around and erupted to the surface in a pattern of dozens of lightning bolts.

I didn't need to stare at the mark. I knew what it meant. Knew it from the moment I touched her and wild energy erupted from the contact.

I knew *exactly* what it meant.

We had all grown up with the stories of the wolves and wolf mates.

Every wolf had a mate, though not every wolf was lucky enough to find them. The moon goddess blessed each shifter with the marks so that they would be able to recognize the other half of their soul. She was my fated mate, my only. I would get no other.

How?

How could she be my soulmate?

A soulmate was supposed to be my true equal.

I looked at this shivering, scrawny thing in front of me. It seemed impossible that the moon had even chosen her as an acceptable vessel for the wolf. Almost as impossible as the fact that this weak thing was deemed an appropriate exchange for my brother in the first place. I was somehow supposed to believe that my one true love was this girl?

It didn't make any sense.

A soft voice cut through my thoughts.

"I accept your rejection." Sofia would not look at me. She licked her lips, eyes darting to the hallways, as if she couldn't wait to get away from me. "We can just keep quiet about this. We never have to tell anyone."

Rejection?

When had I rejected her?

I stepped right into her space, enjoying the way she shivered as she stepped back, pressing herself into the bricks. I slammed my palm against the wall by her side, boxing her in.

I moved in close enough to let the wolf peer out and inspect her.

Her eyes were dark, and they widened as I leaned into her.

At close proximity, her smell unhinged the beast within me. A smell that curved around the wolf's nose, twisting straight through his skull, driving him to insanity.

Within my wolf, something snapped.

Something dark and wild that had no interest in human rules. Disobedient. Feral and unrestrained. Breaking his control. Something that pulsed with a desire so hot, it heated through my veins. My wolf prowled within me, a beast in a frail skin cage, lunging at the bars, fighting to escape, to rip his way free and get to his mate.

The predator within my wolf demanded that I take this girl, as if she were nothing more than prey to be hunted down. The wolf wanted her in his arms, claiming those plush lips. He had to get closer to her. Had to back her all the way against something solid and feel her.

He was close enough to discern the exact flavor of the honey between her thighs. He wanted nothing else.

Luckily, I was more than just a dumb animal.

I clenched my fist until my nails pierced through the skin of my palm, allowing the pain to ground me. The sharp sting cut through the fog of lust in my mind, allowing me to make sense of her words.

"Hide this? Is that what you think is going to happen? You think you're getting away from me?"

"You don't even like me." Sofia gulped. I watched the gentle dip of her slender neck.

"What does that mean? You think that you know my desires better than I do? You think that you can tell me what I want?" I moved closer, cutting through the space between us. One half-step more and her hips would be around mine.

She was right. I didn't like her.

She was a sulking outsider who had wormed her way into my family. For years they had all had to suffer through her presence. Act like this treaty was something normal. Like she was some sort of adequate replacement for my *real* sibling.

Whatever ideas my wolf had gotten into his dumb animal brain, Sofia was not even my type.

But she was mine.

"I can't let the others know," Sophia practically whispered.

She wanted to hide her gift? What? Was she in denial or something?

It didn't matter. From this close, the scent of the wolf was obvious. I could smell the wild musk of her animal. Though new and faint, the scent of it nevertheless clung to her.

I held a strand of her hair, running my fingers down the fine silky texture of it. "You won't be able to hide what you are. Not for long."

She closed her eyes at the contact. Whether to block out the moment, or to relish it, I didn't know.

"Let's get something straight." I laced my fingers through the long locks, tugging down on her hair to force her to meet my gaze. Holding her in place. "Whether you like it or not, you are my soulmate. If I find that you let someone touch what's mine, I will disembowel them. Do you understand?"

Her mouth fell open in surprise. Was a denial on the tip of her lips? Was she going to say that I couldn't do that? Of course I could.

I'm the son of the alpha. Who was going to stop me?

"Don't worry. I would never willingly let you or any of your wolves touch me." Sofia blinked rapidly.

What? What was going on?

Won't let me touch her?

Shouldn't her wolf feel the pull? Mine had felt an instant attraction.

Even I could admit it. Though her human form was feeble, Sofia was far from ugly. That was the entire point of soulmates. Sex and attraction. The offspring of a soul-mated pair were far more likely to produce the next generation of wolves.

My jaw was clenched tight as I tried to force down the snarl that threatened to rip free. Did she mean to deny me my blessing? Did she plan to fight against the power of the moon, the force of nature itself?

Sofia stared at a fixed point on the far wall as her whole body went rigid. "If you're going to do it, just do it already."

The scent of her fear hung in the air. Sour and acidic. My wolf froze at the stench of it. He didn't know what was going on. He wanted to nuzzle at his mate or turn over on his belly and show her that he was not a threat.

None of that wolf stuff would help now. Sofia was too new; the change in her was still raw. The wolf and human intentions would be all mixed up for her.

"I'm not going to force you to do anything," I hissed, narrowing my eyes at her.

How dare she insinuate that I was nothing more than some lowlife? That I would resort to taking my mate unwillingly.

"Then let me go." Her voice shook, and moisture gathered in the corners of her eyes.

I cocked my head, trying to locate the exact source of

the fear that laced through her body, holding all her muscles tight.

Did she really feel nothing? Not a hint, not a tiny shadow of the waves of lust that were threatening to drown me?

Why was she afraid of me? I'd never hurt her. Before tonight, I'd never even touched her.

I could smell the swirls of carbon dioxide as our breaths mingled together. Her lips were soft pink, perfectly formed and close enough I could practically taste them.

"I'm not done with you," I growled, even as I released my hold on Sofia, letting her go.

Because you're mine.

The moment I stepped away from her, Sofia pushed past me and made a run for it.

It took everything in me to stop the wolf from running after her. She had just provided a predator with the most intoxicating chase. The thrill of the hunt was mixed in with the scent of her musk, the sound of her panting as she ran away.

I forced myself to let her run. To get far from my wolf, before he lost control and did something to make her really fear him.

None of this was happening the way that the stories said it would.

My cock strained against my trousers, painfully hard. The smell of my mate was all around me, and the certainty that she wanted nothing to do with me.

How had this gotten all fucked up already?

3

SOFIA

I barely got the lid of the toilet open before hurling up all the remnants of last night's dinner into it. Acid stung the back of my throat as I hung over the porcelain rim, gagging. I kept going until I had nothing left in me, sitting there huddled in my own mess, exhausted.

What if Aaron came after me? It wasn't like he didn't know where I lived. His room was only just around the corridor.

I shivered at the memory of his muscular arms boxing me in. I knew Aaron was big, but then again, he had never quite gotten so close to me. It was one thing to know that he was fit, and quite another to experience all those muscles tensing and flexing as he held me in place. Overpowering me.

Something in my belly fluttered at the thought of that. It wasn't fair. I didn't ask for this. I didn't ask to be attracted to him. Why did my stupid body have to betray me like this?

It didn't matter if I was attracted to him. I could never let him touch me. He was the heir to the Stonevalley wolves. How could I sleep with the enemy? How could I let their bloodline mix with mine?

How could this happen?

It wasn't like I never thought about having a mate. I just assumed it would never happen to me.

I was sure that he was just going to reject me right off the bat.

The experience was locked in my memory. From the moment he looked at the brand on his palm and then looked up at me, every single muscle in his entire body tensed. His jaw tightened as he clenched his teeth. He looked *dangerous,* like a bull lowering his horns, bracing himself for the charge. His eyes narrowed at the sight of me as they had done many times throughout the years before when he had accused me of ridiculous things. The man thought I had schemes to spy on his family or something, when I wanted exactly nothing to do with his family.

When I had accepted his rejection, he'd given me a look like I was a crazy person. Like something as drastic as breaking a soulmate bond simply was not *done.*

I got up from the rim of the toilet seat and considered leaving traces of sick on me in case Aaron decided to come follow me and hash things out between the two of us.

The smell of bile threatened to gag me again. I turned on the sink, scrubbing my face and lathering up with my jasmine-scented hand soap, as if I could bury this traumatic experience with floral toiletries.

What if I rejected *him*?

There was no way in hell Aaron would take that lying down. He'd make my life miserable. If I thought living here was bad before, just wait until his spoiled majesty got denied something he clearly felt entitled to.

How could I live here, breathing the same air as my rejected mate?

Mine.

The possessive voice of my wolf didn't like this train of thought. Didn't like it at all.

How could I do this to her? I couldn't take her away from her mate. The moon never gave a second soulmate bond. Some wolves held back from relationships at all, waiting for the moment when they found their soulmate. I couldn't just think about my own needs; I would be depriving my wolf. Forcing her to live life alone and further isolating her from the pack here.

What was I going to do?

What if he told everyone about me, about the fact that I was now a wolf?

Or what if he came for me?

I might not be able to sort through all the scents through my wolf nose, but I could tell that though he didn't like me, Aaron was aroused. The scent of his desire was deep and earthy, and my lower belly flooded with warmth in response. If I hadn't told him off, he seemed like he'd have been more than happy to fuck me right against that brick wall, out in the open.

My traitorous body heated at the thought of that.

But the night faded into early morning, and he did not come. I was left alone to stew in worry, laying in my bed until the soft morning light hardened into day, anticipating and dreading the moment that I'd see him again.

The next morning, I felt weariness down to my very

bones. My whole body had been ripped apart and rearranged in the transformation. All of my skin faintly burned, and everything from my muscles to my bones was tender. Even my cashmere blankets chafed against my skin.

But at least Aaron had left me alone.

Biting back a groan, I pushed myself up to my feet. If I had told someone that I had turned, I'd probably be allowed a day to myself to heal.

If I wanted to keep my wolf hidden, it was even more important than usual to follow my normal routine.

I got out of my bed and to my feet gingerly.

The alpha demanded that I take lessons, same as the rest of the noble's children. Though combat training lessons had ceased long ago, given up as a lost cause on me, I still had the basic curriculum: lupine history and deportment, alpha politics, biologics and astrology.

At the very least, my classes were scheduled time away from Aaron. He had already completed his lesson requirements a few years before.

I managed to drag my sorry self to class just a minute before the lessons began and froze at the entranceway. My normal spot in the back corner of the class was taken today. Sitting in my chair, Robert Ingolf III smirked at me.

I hesitated for only a moment before taking the last available space, the seat directly in front of Robert.

"Whore," he hissed at me.

Within me, my sleeping wolf roused herself, shaking off sleep. She sniffed the emotions in the air and bared her fangs.

I didn't bother to reply. Feeling this drained had its perks, leaving me too tired to muster up anger.

It was not like this was my first run in with Robert anyway. He just wanted to get a rise out of me. Usually, I would whisper back at him to shut up, or that I hoped he would drown, or something. I'd never tried ignoring him. Maybe it would make him lose interest.

I opened my notebook instead. Professor Rendall drew the Lupus constellation and listed out its boundaries. I copied them down on my chart, sluggishly adding the zodiac connections and moon phases, and their impact on subconscious emotions.

"I can smell your rotten cunt from here, river whore," Robert said, in a voice too quiet for the professor to hear, but just loud enough for another classmate to look up at and smirk at me. I could feel the eyes of my peers on me. Taunting me. Daring me to fight back, to take them all on and get beaten down, again.

I wanted to curl back under my covers and sleep. Between transforming and bonding with my soulmate, I didn't have the energy to fight. Pretending that I couldn't hear a thing, I ducked my head into my notebook and wrote down the lesson with all the vigor of a drowning slug.

After the lesson, it took me a couple of minutes to realize something was wrong. I was stacking my notebooks, forcing my strung-out limbs to cooperate.

The classroom was empty. I was alone, but it was too quiet, and the air felt tense. I threw the rest of my stuff into my leather bag and stood up.

As fast as I could, I stalked out of the room, heading to the stairway. To hell with my personal schedule and people's suspicions. I had to get out of here.

A sharp pain jammed into my stomach, knocking the air out of me.

Robert's face leered down at me.

He kicked me.

The impact of the blow catapulted me backward, until

my hip slammed against a stone window ledge. Trying to stop myself from sliding down, I turned to clutch at the glass panes.

Rough hands pushed hard against my shoulder blades as a heavy body crowded into my space.

"This is all you're good for," Robert whispered into my ear as he pressed against me. Something hard poked against my back and my stomach churned in disgust.

Oh, hell no.

My wolf snarled viciously as her strength burned through me, and claws burst out of my fingertips.

Twisting out of his hold, I swiped with fingers ending in deadly points to tear and rip the skin across his chest.

He jerked away, which saved him from my claws ripping out his throat.

Without stopping to hurl insults, or leave him bloodier, I pushed away from Robert and ran.

4

AARON

I had been trying to give Sofia more time—time to recover from her first wolf transformation, time to process what it would mean to have a soulmate, when pressure burned across my stomach. I hunched over, pressing against the sensation that cut into my muscles.

What the hell?

On my way to head over to the restroom to figure out what was happening to me, pain shot through my hip in a sharp burst that I felt all the way to my bone. Instead of a bruise under my shirt, I found a red mark blooming over my skin with the same lightning pattern as the soulmark on my palm.

"Fuck."

Sofia.

I was running before I had the conscious thought to do so.

My wolf had me hurtling through the corridors and up curved staircases. I was moving before I ever recognized that I was heading to Sofia's room.

Wait. Didn't she go to class?

My wolf was half-frenzied. It was faster to follow the lead of the wolf than the fight it would take to turn him in the direction of Sofia's class. I would be working against primal instincts urging me to move faster. Instincts screaming at me that my mate had been hurt. Had to get to her. Had to protect. To move.

I didn't stop when I got to Sofia's door. Calling on my lupine strength, I used my shoulder as a battering ram. The thin metal of the lock didn't stand a chance against the strength of a wolf shifter.

I burst into Sofia's room, distantly registering the clatter of the lock as it fell to the floor.

Sofia locked her wide-eyed gaze on me, and the stench of pain and tears flooded my nose. Tear trails stained both sides of her cheeks.

My wolf wanted to burst free, destroy whatever was threatening my mate. I clenched my fists as wolf nails burst through me, piercing into skin.

We need to figure out what happened.

My wolf backed down, though he still prowled within me, close to the surface.

I stalked across the room to reach her, and she... flinched. I stilled, stopping in my tracks. She was still afraid of me. Why did Sofia have such a low opinion of me? I would never put my hands on her in anger. Not before when she was just a slinking outcast, and certainly not now that I knew she was my soulmate.

"Who did this to you?" My words were practically a snarl.

"What are you talking about?" She broke eye contact, eyes flicking to the door, planning how she was going to get away again.

Was she denying what happened? Did she dare lie right to my face?

I crossed the remaining distance between us. I trailed a finger along her stomach. "So if I lifted your blouse right here, I wouldn't see any bruise." My hand drifted along her trim waist to her hip. As I rested my hand lightly where I had felt her pain bloom, Sofia winced. "Tell me who hurt you."

"It doesn't matter." Sofia refused to look me in the eye, and it made my wolf anxious, even as it pissed me off.

Didn't matter? What the hell was wrong with this girl? She was in a not insignificant amount of pain.

"You're my mate." The words were out of my mouth before I could hold back, before I could remember that this was all new to her, and I was trying to give her time to adjust. "Any attack on you is a direct challenge to the authority of the pack hierarchy."

"But he had no idea that I'm yours, and it's better for both of us if it stays that way." Sofia turned away from me as she insisted on secrecy. "If it's Robert today, it will be Mark, or Evan or Sam tomorrow. You can't stop all of them from hating me."

So many fucking men were after what was mine. Robert. Mark. Evan. Sam. Each one of them was a dead man if I saw them so much as look at her. This girl was driving me crazy, with her secrets and her intoxicating scent, coating every inch of her room.

As her smell drew me in, I stepped closer. I placed my palm against the column of her neck, stroking her soft skin. "None of them would dare if they knew you're my mate. Even if they hate you." I wanted to mark her neck, coating her in my kisses and my scent so that no one would put a finger on her again.

I inhaled deeply. She smelled like jasmine and desire, newly bloomed lupine, the forest... and fresh blood.

I grasped the source of the smell, taking her hand in my own. She wasn't wounded, with fresh blood. No, the source of the blood hadn't come from Sofia at all. It must have been from her attacker. Close up, I could smell the pheromones within the blood, the sharp spike of arousal.

Whoever did this wanted her and was willing to hurt her to get what he wanted.

The source of the blood was beneath her fingernails. So, she didn't let him.

"You fought him." I stroked against her fingertips, noting how Sofia went completely still. I leaned closer to whisper right next to the shell of her ear, "Good girl."

Sofia gasped, but she didn't try to pull away.

I wanted to tug her against my chest and feel all of her soft curves pressed against me. I wanted to let my fingers trail down, to explore all the hidden depths of her body. I wanted all of her.

But Sofia was weak from her first change. After my first lunar shift, I had been on bed rest for three days. Besides, she was injured. I could smell the bruises pooling under her skin as easily as I could smell her pheromones, a heady mix of fear and desire. No. I would give her space.

"If you are going to insist on hiding what you are to me, then I am going to insist on things as well." Reluctantly, I backed away from her. Sofia turned to look at me with a grimace. As if bracing herself against my nefarious plans. "If you want to hide our connection, I will have to keep close. I'll follow you and make sure this doesn't happen again."

"No, you can't."

"No? I'm not going to allow my wolf to go feral and

endanger the lives of my pack because you want to hide what you are. Because you can't keep yourself safe."

Sofia still insisted on keeping me at a distance. She wanted her secrets, not that what we had between us was a secret we would be able to keep. But I would indulge her, for now. In time Sofia would learn her place.

SOFIA

How did that old saying go? Familiarity was supposed to breed contempt? Yeah, that wasn't working out for me.

Aaron, true to his word, began to stick close.

I caught glimpses of him as I walked from one class to another. Even when I couldn't see him, I could smell his presence. His smell was the cooling scent of cedarwood and the citrusy hint of bergamot. My wolf preened every time she sensed that he was near. If she could do it, she would want to live in his scent. Lap it up. Swim in it.

This attraction wasn't fair.

The last time Aaron and I spoke was when he barged into my room. Too soon after my change, he had caught me vulnerable, with newly grown skin and bones. He'd just seen the blood on my hands and realized that I had fought my way away from Robert. He had leaned too close and not close enough. Hovering just out of reach, as his lips stopped within kissing distance. Whispering words that echoed within my skull.

Good girl.

I wanted to howl that I didn't do it for him. I had fought Robert because that bastard didn't deserve to touch me. He polluted the balance of pheromones in the air with the stink of his presence. I would have attacked any male that touched me without my permission.

But was that even true anymore? When Aaron murmured into my ear, I was frozen. If he had moved closer to me, what would I have done? It was like I was forgetting myself. Forgetting my roots and my history.

This land was drenched in the blood of my people. The stench of wrongness, of something other, something that was most definitely not *pack*. It clung to the leaves of plants, festering on every surface and lingering in the very air. The scent of the enemy pressed in from all around.

I was young when the peace talks were drafted between the two packs. Generations of hatred were supposed to be ended neatly with the sacrifice of two children barely in their teenage years. The feud had passed down the blood-line for generations, with constant tension and outbreaks of outright war. If it hadn't been for the decline in wolves, the peace talks would have never been drafted.

The beast within me seemed to cock an ear at that, listening, trying to understand my human reasons. My wolf didn't understand why I was here. Why was I torn away from the pack and living amongst people who were not my own?

What would my pack think of me now, half panting over the heir to the Stonevalley alpha? How could I let myself betray my people? I hadn't seen my family in years, but how could I ever face them again?

Aaron was my enemy.

No matter how delicious he smelled.

AARON

Mother sipped at her tea delicately, gesturing for me to take a seat. She had placed a tray of fine tea as well as a charcuterie board in front of me, as if this was some sort of social call.

Mother's tea parlor was more delicately arranged than the rest of the castle. Soft light from crystal chandeliers illuminated gold leaf crown molding. Priceless Turkish cotton rugs were scattered about to catch all the crumbs from her biscotti and crumpets.

I sat gingerly at the edge of her plush velvet guest chair. The color was a rich violet which faded abruptly to a dark blue as I strained my wolf senses, listening. I couldn't hear any disturbances in the conversations around Sofia. Nothing but her professor lecturing. The longer I spent monitoring my mate, the more I caught snatches of nasty conversations. Her classmates. Wolves. Regular humans. They all thought that they could get away with harassing her. The list kept on growing, though there were a handful more aggressive than the others that I was keeping my eye on.

Why hadn't she ever said anything?

All of it would stop if they knew that she was mine. Keeping quiet about our connection was grating away at my peace of mind.

Sofia was safe. For now, that was all that mattered. I grasped the delicate bone china roughly and took a swig of the herbal tea that was meant to be savored.

"Your father mentioned that your performance has been lacking recently." Mother took another sip of tea, pursing her lips as if it were the flavor and not the turn of conversation that suddenly soured the air.

I'd been waiting for this talk since the moment I'd started keeping an eye out for Sofia. Of course the alpha would notice a decline in my duties. He was always monitoring me, tracking the progress of his heir. Instead of telling me himself, the old man sent Mother.

Criticizing me was a delicate matter, and the alpha wouldn't approach me directly for this. He wouldn't do anything that could potentially harm the transfer of power from alpha to heir. No. Why would he do that when he could send Mother to do his dirty work?

Mother stared at me expectantly, and I sighed.

How could I explain what I was doing without her requesting I change? I couldn't stop my vigil on Sofia. My mate wasn't safe. I couldn't lie to my mother; she'd scent that a mile away.

There was no other option for me than the truth.

I unbuttoned the clasp at the top of my gloves, and mother's eyes widened as I tugged at each finger, loosening it. I pulled off the glove, revealing my soulmark. The swirls which started as angry red welts now looked more like an odd birthmark, or a somewhat faded tattoo.

"Oh, darling, that's wonderful." Her eyes were large

with unshed tears as she clasped both of her hands around mine. "No wonder you have been distracted; this explains everything. When can I meet her?"

I wanted to yank the glove back on. I did *not* need this reminder of how the soulbond was supposed to go. Damn that gleam in my mother's eyes. She thought I was distracted for the past few weeks because I was off making her grandchildren.

"Oh," she gasped suddenly. "We need to organize your official bonding ceremony. I'll need you to find out from your mate what flowers she prefers for the decorations. Also her birthstone, to get an order sent to the jewelers immediately. I can handle the invitations and seat arrangements if you are still too busy."

I placed Mother's favorite porcelain teacup back on the tray with care to stop myself from smashing it. This conversation was worse than a needle piercing into the bed of my fingernails. I had to set her straight on the reality of my soulbond before she jumped to any more conclusions.

"She doesn't want anything to do with me."

"Don't be ridiculous." Mother smiled up at me. "It must simply be a misunderstanding between the two of you. You are the heir to the alpha of the Stonevalley pack, not some beta or useless omega male. Any wolf would be proud to have you as a mate."

My chest felt tight as my pulse began to quicken. Mother wasn't listening to me. She wouldn't unless I told her everything.

"No, she's not. It's Sofia."

Mother opened her mouth in surprise before closing it tightly. All of her enthusiasm seemed to drain away. "That's not possible."

"I assure you, it is."

The silence from Mother was damning. She tapped a finger rapidly against the table and shifted in her seat uncomfortably.

"This is not what your father and I wanted for you," Mother sighed, shaking her head. "But if Sofia doesn't want you... If that's not something you can change, there is still time for you to claim a more suitable wolf."

Another wolf?

Someone that didn't have that bewitching scent of jasmine, a scent that both riled the beast within me and soothed him? The thought of replacing my soulmate with someone else, some fucking stranger, had me seething.

My entire body tensed, and I had to avert my eyes from the concerned look on Mother's face. Force myself to take in steady breaths. Deep breaths. In and out. I had to control myself, or my high-strung wolf would erupt out of my body and rip apart Mother's fine velvet cushions in his drive to protect my mate from this new intangible threat.

"I don't want some other wolf." My voice deepened until it was practically a growl. "I want her."

"For gods' sakes, she's your sister."

After all the stories Mother had told me about the soul-bound wolves, how could she even suggest this? My very first thought after learning I was a shifter, as soon as I could think through the pain of it, was the relief that having a wolf meant having a *mate*. Knowing that someone out there was more than my perfect match. A mate was the other half of my soul, chosen by the goddess herself. And now what? My own mother thought I could just reject her? That somehow, some other choice was better than the will of the goddess. Better for me than my very soul's twin?

I was practically vibrating with tension. Every inch of my body was tight, as this conversation was pulling me apart. I hadn't realized that I took for granted Mother's support until that was suddenly taken away.

"No."

I was done with this conversation.

Standing abruptly, I flexed and relaxed my fist, letting the bite of my own nails ground me, as I fought to get back the control that was slipping away from me. When I finally trusted my voice to speak, I turned to Mother, who had grown pale.

"I have never considered Sofia to be my sister."

7

SOFIA

Most nights I got a dinner tray sent up to my room, but I had to put in an official appearance once a week or more in order to avoid suspicion. For tonight, I dressed in a simple silk cowl neck dress in sage green. I paired my gown with pearl drop earrings. The look was both minimalist enough to avoid attention, and sophisticated enough to avoid censure.

We were monsters dressed in our best. To those who lived in the Stonevalley castle without the body of the wolf, perhaps all of this seemed truly genteel. But as someone who had felt the burning hunger, that raw unbridled power of the wolf, these clothes were nothing short of ridiculous.

I slipped on the long silk gloves that stopped just past the elbow, hiding my soulmark. The mark had faded somewhat. It was less of an angry raised welt and more of a faint discoloration on the skin. Yet, whenever my wolf rose to the surface, I could feel the animal heat through the mark—a carnal longing so strong that my skin became warm to the touch.

In the past, I had always found gloves annoying. But

tonight, I was glad that formal dinner attire favored a history of copying the trends of the alpha. Wolves in power typically covered their hands to avoid triggering a soul match during formal dinners. It was not uncommon for wolves finding their soulmates to lose control and consummate immediately. Obviously, that would put the rest of the guests off dinner and put an early end to polite conversation. For already matched wolves, the marks themselves were considered a private affair. I was just glad that I never rebelled and went without them now that I had actual marks to hide.

The moment that I walked into the dining hall, I could feel his eyes on me. I swallowed, breathing in steady, calming breaths. It wouldn't do for Aaron to smell the hormonal warfare his gaze wrought upon me. Heat pooled deep in my belly as my heart beat faster. It was as if messages from my mind and my body were misfiring. Or perhaps it was pure rebellion. My body didn't give a damn that Aaron was my enemy.

Only when I was certain that I had myself under control did I look up to meet his gaze. As soon as I did, Aaron tapped the high table, clearly signaling me over. My heart sank to somewhere below my stomach.

I was technically required to sit at the high table, though over the years I had drifted away. No one had ever said anything when I sat with the lesser nobles—the betas and their families. It was easier to be ignored there, and I didn't want to be on anyone's radar.

Now Aaron's signal had put me in the spotlight. If anyone had paid attention and saw me ignore the direct instruction of the heir to the alpha, there would be hell to pay. There was no way that I'd be able to simply slip out of the public eye. Maybe not ever again.

I maneuvered over to the high table and took an empty seat at the end, ignoring the open seat by Aaron. Though he had the power to move me to the high table, it didn't mean that I had to sit anywhere near him. Why the hell did he want me to sit here anyway? What kind of point was he trying to make? That he could force me to follow the rules everyone was happy to have ignored for years?

Aaron hadn't said it directly, but he was trying to figure out who attacked me. I often caught glimpses of him nearby whenever I switched from one classroom to the other. He never did anything, but his eyes would linger on my body, with a gaze heated enough that in all fairness my clothes should have burst into flames.

The physical draw to him was only growing stronger the longer I ignored it. If this desire for him was a tangible thing, I'd rip it straight out of my body, dig it up from where it settled into my bones. This attraction was poison. If only I could, I would extricate it and free myself.

The high table seated the alpha's immediate family as well as the most dominant generals. Aaron's mother, the Lady Ragnolf, sat at the head of the table. Regal and poised, her blonde hair was piled high in an elaborate braided updo. To her left, sat Dagmar, Aaron's gruff uncle. He talked to no one and dug into his meal as if it was his full time job. At his side General Albertsen glared at me in pure narrow-eyed suspicion. I dropped my eyes demurely, hoping the submissive gesture would break off his attention. The last thing I needed was an old war hero to start sniffing too close to my affairs.

Next to me sat Kara Ragnolf, Aaron's only cousin, who glanced at me once dismissively with a tight lip. She turned away from me as if she scented something foul in the air.

Fair enough. The murderous Stone stench was all over

her, and the only thing that stopped me from gagging was the long exposure to it. But I couldn't remember if Kara was one of the wolves, or someone mimicking them for favor.

Careful not to let my nostrils flare, I inhaled deeply, catching the floral residue of her shampoo, the rose toner of her skin care routine.

The scent of wolf was an unmistakable musk with an edge, like something spicy, something wild. Like the hint of wind coursing through rough fur in the forest. Like the sweat of the hunt, and hot panting breaths through pointed fangs.

On Kara, I smelled nothing but human. Despite her dislike of me, Kara was safe enough. She didn't have the power of the wolf behind her bite to harm me. Nor the heightened senses to be able to tell that I was a creature so much more powerful than she.

Though those around me had lively conversations, for me dinner was a quiet affair. I cut the chicken on my plate with care, though my heightened senses zeroed in on the crisp layer of skin, roasted to perfection. The proportions of fresh ground pepper, paprika, and the dried thyme and basil. I bit a small morsel delicately off my fork rather than grabbing the meat with both hands to rip a chunk right off the bone.

Halfway through my third course, some liquid splashed all the way down the front of my gown. A crisp white Riesling, a lovely dessert wine, and now I was somehow drenched in it. Part of the drink splashed onto my plate, ruining the rest of my meal.

Kara hid a smirk behind the palm she held over her mouth. If I wasn't sitting right next to her, her expression would have looked like a shocked surprise. The glass by her plate was toppled over. The malice in the cold sting of her pretty blue eyes and the faint scent of anger in the air around her let me know that this was no accident.

"How clumsy of me," she said in a soft voice for only me to hear.

The wolf considered the fragile human who watched us with a sly smirk on her face, wondering if her blood would be enough to cool the rage simmering within her. A growl echoed from within the confines of my body, loud enough that I was shocked that no one else at the party reacted to the sound. It came from anger buried so deep, I thought it was lost and locked away. Reverberating through every inch of me.

I stood up, though etiquette demanded that I stay until the alpha finished his meal. There was a limit to my patience, and I couldn't trust myself to remain peaceful at the table. Not while dripping and withholding my wolf from a revenge sweeter than the wine staining my favorite outfit.

Conversations stilled to quiet as I passed tables by. Until I completely exited the dining hall. Before I shut the wooden double door behind me, I could hear pointed conversations whispered excitedly.

I hesitated by the door for a moment, debating whether I wanted to rush to my room or sneak down to the kitchen to see if Martha would take pity on me and serve me a plate of dessert before I turned in for the night.

The double doors opened and out stepped Aaron.

It was the first time I had been this close to him since he'd broken into my room. Aaron wasted no time approaching me and grasping my shoulders. "Are you all right?"

"Drink spilled on me," I muttered, breaking eye contact

as he searched into my expression intently. Checking to see what was wrong.

Even looking away, I could still feel the heat in his bright blue eyes.

Dear gods.

The longer I stayed away from this man, the harder it was to resist the pull to him. Was this due to the soulmate bond? Was it causing all these physical reactions within me, trying to force the connection between us?

No, it wasn't all just chemicals firing off in my brain. Aaron had always been attractive. It was more than the simple fact that he was blonde and broad and muscular. He was regal and fierce. Aaron had unmistakable authority in his bearings. The power, the dominance of the bloodline of the alpha was alive in every one of his coiled muscles, present in each of his precise movements.

Yes, he had always been attractive, but also far away and safely off limits.

Though Aaron made no move closer, he was not unaffected. He stared at my dress with a somewhat dazed expression. Not like he was seeing the stain I pointed out, and more like he wanted to rip all that fabric off of me.

"Why did you make me move tables?"

"How do you expect me to keep you safe from across the room?" His eyes were hooded with desire and tended to linger on my mouth. My pulse leaped at his proximity, as every cell in my body ignored the warnings in my mind telling me that this was wrong and wanted nothing else but for this man to press closer and claim me.

Aaron leaned closer to me, like he wasn't aware that he was doing it. I gasped as a stupid curiosity came over me, demanding to know how it would feel if he was closer.

What would happen next if I let him press his lips against my own.

"Goodnight," I blurted out stupidly as I moved back.

Aaron made a half step closer to me and started to raise his hand to reach out to me. He abruptly stopped, as if changing his mind. "Good night," he repeated in a hoarse voice.

I could feel his eyes on me as I made my retreat back to my room, and my wolf cursed every step, whining like I was making a mistake.

What the fuck was happening to me?

Despite being one of the stone wolves, despite the war that was written into our very genetic code, Aaron didn't smell like the enemy to me any longer.

He smelled amazing. Absolutely good enough to eat.

8

AARON

What was the point of being the heir to the alpha if all it meant was that I had to sort through a mountain of paperwork? It was a waste of all the brute strength of the wolf.

After my last conversation with Mother, I realized that neglecting my duties indefinitely was not sustainable. Daily reports piled up. Transactions requiring my approval were all delayed. So instead of tracking my mate, who was facing daily bullying, or worse, I was in my chancellery, reading over backed up documents that somehow all required my signature. The process was tedious.

I paused over a report on the Edgeriver wolves. Scouts confirmed a sighting of the new wolf added to their territory. Confirmed male, twice as large as a normal non-shifter wolf and bone-white. I placed the report back on his desk with a sigh. There was no question about it. The description matched my own exactly. The new wolf was Erik. My twin brother.

I drummed my fingers against the desk, straining to read between the lines, searching for any hint to the questions burning in my mind. Questions I'd had in the back of my mind since the trade years ago. Questions best left unanswered.

How was Erik taking to being a wolf?

How was he being treated in the Edgeriver pack?

I didn't know what would be worse—if Erik was treated well and thought of the river wolves as his new family, or if he wasn't and didn't.

I had known that this was coming. Known since my own wolf had awakened that it was more than likely that my brother's would awaken as well. With the addition of Erik, that made three new wolves from the river wolves in the years since the trade. In the same time frame, the Stonevalley pack gained one wolf. Me.

Well, two now. At least unofficially, as Sofia was off the records. The first thing I had done was skim through the paperwork for any mention of her. She was added to the official registry. Dead last, as if she was some afterthought, with her designation set to human.

The lack of new wolves was the single greatest unspoken source of tension, putting everyone, human and wolves alike, on edge. The pressure built with each full moon with no new members added to the pack. It was only a few generations back that nearly every child born into the tribe could expect to shift under the first full moon after coming of age.

The alpha had increased training for the younger generation. The fact that Sofia had been allowed to withdraw from the majority of those extra training lessons yet still became a wolf revealed that his plan was useless.

Though I had been blind to the way others in the pack had treated Sofia before the soulbond, the others would have to react differently when they saw that she was a wolf.

Our numbers were too low to shun her, despite her back-ground. I had to believe that some bonds ran deeper than prejudice. What hope did Sofia and I have otherwise?

A name on the corner of one paper caught my eye. One of the names of the nastier bullies I had been monitoring. Robert Ingolf, the third of his name, was born from a direct pedigree of seven generations of wolf shifters. All boasting strong beta lines and close alpha connections. He was one of the younger generation who would boast to whoever was around to hear it that he could sense that he had a wolf within him. He was one among the most recent group that went out with Sofia during the full moon corresponding to the vernal equinox. He had not turned.

I suspected that he was the one who had attacked my mate. The only thing that was keeping his filthy lungs still breathing was my desire to see if he had any connections. A hunch, nagging at me, suggested that he wasn't the only one.

I skimmed through the report. Reading through mentions of a misdemeanor. Apparently, Robert was given a warning for wandering too close to the armory. The notes states that Robert gave the excuse that he was stepping out to the courtyard to check on the state of the moon.

Right.

Why just a warning? He got no consequence whatso-ever. Robert was banking on the reputation bought by his legacy. His record was spotless, besides this one incident.

Didn't anyone question the fact that he was out at ten? Right at the change of shift. What the hell was he doing at the armory? It was what the alpha deemed the war room. Filled with all the non-training weapons. Consistently sharpened and at the ready, waiting for the first sign of war resuming with the Edgeriver tribe. Any number of the things in that room could harm Sofia.

I clenched my eyes shut, bracing against the table in a wordless scream. Pain. An intense burst of pain laced through my neck, so sharp I couldn't think through it. Worse than the pain of having the wolf rip through my body, worse than having all the bones broken apart and shifted. My neck and shoulder felt raw, as if burned completely away by acid. I grasped at the area, prodding it.

Was I shot? What the fuck was happening?

I saw nothing but a pattern, one that I recognized. It was a set of swirls in the same pattern as my soulmark now pulsing in a deep red against my neck.

Fuck.

This pain wasn't happening to me. This was just a shadow of it.

Someone was trying to murder Sofia.

9

SOFIA

My classes had been generally quiet for the past few weeks, so it was no surprise to me when I went to my assigned telescope and found it broken. No matter what I did, I could not get it to focus. The image was too blurry to get the accurate reading for the star chart that was due at the end of the week.

I looked around the room at all the equipment being used. It wasn't hard to imagine what would happen if I went to my classmates and asked them to borrow theirs. Same thing that always happened when I'd ask for anything—a pencil, the homework, if that chair was taken—my presence was met with blank stares at best, and at other times harsh laughter. Their rejection wasn't even something I registered anymore. An unpleasant fact of nature, like bad weather. Unavoidable.

I wanted not to care. But there was a good chance that skipping this assignment would mean that Professor Hanson would report my progress as incomplete. Which could mean that I would be left taking the entire course over. Again, it would be easier if I didn't care. Did it matter how many years I was left completing academic courses? Sitting through lectures with a new crop of students who would quietly bide their time, waiting for their professor's back to turn. A new class meant a new group of peers who would hate me without provocation.

I sighed, packing my notes together and shouldering my bag. The armory would likely have spares. It was in the south wing of the castle, in the complete opposite direction. But if I left now, I'd have time to borrow a spyglass and finish at least part of my chartwork.

The south wing didn't feel right. As I walked down the stairs to reach the armory, the air was stale. I couldn't scent any guards, though the armory was meant to be under a constant guard. I pulled my shawl tighter around myself. It felt cold, almost unnaturally so. As if the frigid air leaked cold straight into the castle foundation.

I didn't need my wolf growling a warning within me to know that something was wrong. I could feel it in my gut. Casually, carefully, I lowered my arms to the side. I walked at a fast clip, half closing my eyes as I let the wolf senses take over.

Catching a strong scent of dirt and pine needles made my wolf pause. There was something under those other smells. I closed my eyes, letting the wolf take over. The scent was faint, but unmistakable. Human. Someone was hiding their presence under the overpowering scent of pine. But there was something else. Another hidden scent. My nose flared wide, taking it in. The scent was metallic, but hard to place.

Whatever it was, it was wrong. It wasn't safe. And here I was, exposed to the danger of it, surrounded on all sides by people who would see me harmed and turn their heads to smile.

I had to get out of here. Had to warn someone. The scent of pine grew stronger, accompanied by the sound of someone's rapid breaths. Whoever it was sounded excited.

I had already waited too long. Let myself get too distracted by the tool I needed that was in easy reach. Turning, I walked away from the armory as fast as I dared.

Large hands grasped the back of my neck, slamming my face into the stone wall.

And then the pain began.

10

AARON

I prodded the burning pain in my neck, half-shocked when my hand didn't come away coated in blood.

What the fuck was this?

As soon as I realized that something was happening to Sofia, my wolf went feral. He spun around wildly within me, fighting against my body, scratching under my skin, trying to break through my ribs to get out. To go save his mate.

With the intensity of his reaction, I couldn't hold him back. Couldn't warn him that this was a job better left for the nuances of the human mind. Watched him rage and ignore my every attempt to communicate.

I held onto the reins of control, tugging on my mind, tensing and bracing for the moment the wolf would surface and take control.

Within me, my wolf howled, confined within my body as if my flesh were too strong of a prison cell.

Why the hell couldn't my wolf break out of me?

At just like that, the answer of what was happening to Sofia was obvious. I gasped in horror. Tensing all my muscles, I forced myself to my feet. Every part of me shook with rage.

That they would dare.

I stroked my wounds with the promise that soon I would be soothing them with blood. I couldn't wait to feel their blood run beneath my teeth.

But more important than revenge, I had to get to Sofia.

My mate was on the cusp of death. I could feel the echoes of her pain written into my own skin.

11

SOFIA

Against my neck, something was burning. It was like the gentle blessing of the moon, intensified to the power of a supernova and pressed directly against my skin. My body was wired. Reacting. Forced into needing to shift, to transform, but bound in place. The angry hiss of sizzling and popping pressed in loud and too close. In the air was the scent of smoke and burned pork.

It was coming from me.

Within me, my wolf scratched at the skin beneath my ribs, fighting to get out. Fierce as she was, my body was a cage. She couldn't even push free at the edges; her claws pushed against my fingertips and were blocked.

What could do this? What the hell was happening...?

Silver.

That asshole pressed a silver chain into me, and it was charring through my flesh. Forcing the wolf to react, but too intense for her to break through.

Why the fuck would he do this to me? Why did he even have silver? It was contraband of the highest order. Possession of silver was grounds for immediate expulsion from the pack.

"Why?" All the words I couldn't manage to get out settled on the tip of my tongue. *Why do this to me? What do you want? Why me?*

I was speaking to myself more than calling out to my attacker, and not expecting an answer. But he responded.

"Because," he hissed. With that one word, I recognized his voice. After years of sharing classes and learning under the same professors, I finally recognized my classmate. It was Robert, though his scent was smothered in the harsh scents of wet soil and pine. "You don't deserve to be here."

I tried to ask a question, but all that slipped out of my tortured lips was an undignified moan as he pressed the silver deeper against my neck like a brand.

What did he mean? That I didn't deserve to be here? This wasn't my decision. I was chosen to be here. For the truce. For my people.

Robert was using silver against me. So that meant that he knew. He knew that I was a wolf. Knew it—and didn't care.

Something within me bristled at that and raised an ugly head. It was one thing to take a look at me, to see a body that was uncoordinated and not frail exactly, but nothing compared to the other athletic women who bore the blood of wolves. But it was another thing entirely to judge my wolf.

I rammed my elbow into any piece of him that I could find. I heard a satisfying *Oomf* as the sharp blow made contact with his soft underbelly. The blow jostled his arm just enough for me to break away from the burn of silver.

I flexed my fingers, willing my wolf to the surface. I had

just enough time for claws to burst out of the tips of my fingers, arching my arm back, poised to strike.

"No, you don't, bitch," Robert snarled as he slammed me back. The silver wrapped between his fingers burned hotter against my skin. Burning straight into me. Pure agony thudded through every inch of my veins. Worse after my moment of sweet relief.

Smoke emerged from the tips of my fingers where it looked like the claws of my wolf were dissolving. The wolf within me tipped back her head, howling. Not quite understanding what was happening to her. I could sense her limping with her mangled paw. Crying out for her mate.

Robert pressed my arm back with his other hand, twisting it hard until something snapped. I bit down on my lip to hold in a scream. There was no way I would give this overgrown rat the satisfaction. He didn't get to see my pain.

My arm fell to my side loosely. Useless.

Robert grabbed my shaking body and bashed my head against the stone wall with the hand holding the silver. At the impact, white stars dotted my vision. He pushed the chains harder into my skin, pressing the silver in so tight that the tips of his knuckles turned white.

Deep within myself, something snapped. Something that wasn't supposed to break was cracking apart. My wolf whimpered once. One soft, pained sound, and then she was silent.

I couldn't feel her anymore.

Reaching within myself, I sought after her. Needing to feel her. Desperate for a brush of her coarse fur. The sting of her fangs. For anything.

But I couldn't feel her. Not a single trace of her. It was as if my wolf wasn't there at all anymore.

No.

I was numb.

How was that possible? Robert didn't... Did he just destroy my wolf?

As the pain overwhelmed me, I opened my eyes wide. Blinking rapidly. Forcing back the darkness with the sheer force of my will.

It was too much.

I felt myself starting to fade.

Darkness rose in a tide, swirling around the outskirts of my vision. Calling to me. Lulling me. Telling me to drift away. To sleep. To let the pain finally stop.

No.

No, this wasn't the end for me. I wasn't going to die at the grubby hands of Robert Ingolf III.

I scrabbled with my one good hand, letting the tips of my fingers sizzle as the flesh blistered and cracked open at the touch of silver. I fought him anyway, even as it burned. Finding purchase and digging into his skin. With raw, burned hands, I scratched and tore. Curving my fingers, looping them around the burn of the metal. Tugging the chain away from my vulnerable, too damaged neck.

From behind me, I heard a grunt of surprise, and something tearing.

The silver chain fell to the ground as Robert lost his grip on me. I swayed and slid down the stone wall, unable to hold myself up. Collapsing to the floor in a huddle. I fought to hold myself upright. I needed to see what was happening. What Robert was up to. To see how he was going to hurt me next, to gather up my defenses against it. To try and stop it.

I forced myself to breathe deep. I had to be alert.

Something dropped to the ground, slapping against the stone with an odd squelch.

I forced myself to look at it. To use my broken body and fight.

It took me a moment to understand. The round mass of hair, about the size of a bowling ball, was Robert's head... but it was no longer connected to his body.

That was when I realized that someone else had entered the corridor as he crouched down in front of me.

Aaron—with blood splattered across his face and drenching the front of his fine damask shirt—grabbed my chin, peering into my eyes.

12

AARON

He fucking dared.

Adrenaline and rage flowed through me, demanding that I kill him a second time.

My nostrils flared as I forced myself to breathe, to clear my head from the haze of red. I could barely hear through the roar of blood pounding in my ear, with the snarling and feral howling of my wolf.

The blood of the man who did this was not enough to cool the fury threatening to blind me.

A small whimper caught my attention, reshifting my focus completely.

Sophia was huddled on the ground with a dazed expression, lightly grasping the raw wound left behind by the silver. Burns ravaged her delicate swan-like neck. The edges were charred to blackened crisps. I clenched my hands so hard that my nails pierced into my skin.

Why the fuck would he do this?

As gently as I could, I held her chin, looking into her pupils. Which looked even, thank the goddess. No head trauma from when that brute jammed her against stone walls.

The memory of watching that pathetic little worm of a man put his hands on my mate—how he had *hurt* her. I had to watch him slam my soulmate's head against stone and feel the echo of her pain. Watch and do nothing. All while I was just a minute out of reach.

"Aaron?" Her voice, usually proper and crisp, sounded muddled. Faint.

"I'm here."

My voice was rough with all the words I didn't say. That I was here now. That I was sorry. That I should have been there for her, should have been watching.

Her injuries were severe. I could smell the damage that her body had endured. All the chemical cocktails of stress hormones within her. This was bad.

"Hey." I moved my hand along her cheek, brushing along her smooth skin. "You need to shift."

This damage was too severe for her to heal on her own. As soon as she could take on the form of her wolf, her body would be reformed, taking away the brunt of her injuries.

Sofia closed her eyes; a crease of concentration formed between her eyebrows. Her breathing slowed as she turned her attention within herself, reaching out to her wolf.

After a moment, she shook her head. "I can't."

What did it mean if she wasn't able to reach out to her wolf? Could it mean that her injuries were worse than I thought?

I leaned down closer to her, getting to her eye level. "I'm going to pick you up."

I slid my hands under her back, gently supporting the back of her neck. Careful to avoid the raw injuries there, I lifted her into my arms. She was so light.

An image of her came to my mind's eye, of the moment after our soulbound connection sparked. How she ruthlessly denied me. Challenging me. There was so much force to her. I couldn't believe that all that determination, all that willpower, came packaged in this tiny frame.

With Sofia cradled in my arms, I walked as quickly as I could. I had to get her outside. It wasn't quite dark. The light of the sun hadn't fully set, but even the limited moonlight available should give her a boost.

She murmured against me like a newborn kitten, cuddling close. Her head hung listlessly against my chest, and I could feel her breaths shortening against me.

She looked like she was dying.

I swallowed and quickened my steps. Within me, my heart was pounding so hard that I could hear the harsh thudding in my ears, making my head start to spin.

My soulmate was in my arms fading. Burned by silver on my own fucking territory. Burned even though I knew that she was in danger. I knew that people were threatening her. And now she was hurt because I hadn't been paying attention.

If she didn't make it...

I couldn't think about losing her. No. I couldn't think like that. I had to hold it together. For her.

She was still breathing.

As long as I was breathing too, I would fight for her.

The armory wasn't too far from the exits leading out into the forests, and I had never covered the distance over there quicker.

I took her out into a clearing in the woods, in the old growth forest. Soon the first rays of the moon would flood the area.

I laid her down gently on the grass and bent close to her ear to whisper. "Sofia, you need to shift."

"I can't." Her voice was small and pained, and it sounded nothing like her. Where was my fierce girl? My fighter that didn't take any shit from anybody?

"Yes. You can do this," I said in a voice more confident than I felt. "Reach for your wolf."

Sofia closed her eyes, pressing her hand to the center of her chest as if she could reach in if she pushed hard enough and physically grasp at her wolf. Clenching her eyes tight with the strain of it. She concentrated, pulling from deep within herself.

After a moment, she stopped, shaking her head faintly. She seemed to sink lower, as if her last attempt to shift took out too much of the little strength that remained.

"I'm sorry," she murmured.

13

SOFIA

Aaron was kneeling beside me, speaking directly into my ear until it felt like my mind was filled with him. Just him. His voice was low and commanding, practically a growl. "Sofia, you can't give up."

My wolf wasn't just far away. The raw energy that flooded through me pushed her. Washed her away like she was a tsunami. Since the moment of my first shift, I had always been able to feel her. She prowled within me like a second piece of my essence, my very soul. More than the burns I felt in my neck, I felt like some deep sacred part of me had been ripped apart.

How could I explain to him that I hadn't given up? There wasn't anything to give up. Fighting harder to shift wouldn't make a difference. My wolf was gone.

I closed my eyes tight, unable to look at him. Aaron didn't know what he had lost. That his mate was gone. The goddess of the moon did not provide a second chance.

He held my face cupped in both of his large hands. "Sophia, I've watched you stand your own against anyone who's tried to hurt you. You're a fighter. You can do this. I know you can."

I raised my heavy eyelids to the bright blue of his gaze, locked on mine. It was as if I was waking up with new eyes. Like I had been blind. For the first time, I could look at him without first seeing a Stonevalley wolf. An enemy alpha. It was the first time I was really seeing him without all the labels I'd attached to him.

For the first time, I saw just the man.

Staring back at me with a desperate terror in his intense gaze. Scared for me.

He was so close.

With the last of my strength, I leaned up toward him and pressed my lips against his. The touch of his lips was plush and softer than I imagined. For a moment, his mouth was stiff, as if I'd shocked him, before pressing back, hot and feral. His tongue swept into my mouth as I gasped. Sliding against mine.

Echoes of pleasure heated all down my soulmark. My head was swimming with the flavor of him—traces of mint, aged scotch and raw strength. Absolutely delicious. Flooding me with desire.

I could let myself have this once.

From deep within myself, I thought I heard something stirring. Something that had been locked away in some far forgotten corner of my mind.

I slipped away from him with a sigh as my head rang— sounds faded behind the rush of noise, like a roaring wind.

He was saying something. I thought I saw the shape of my name on his lips.

The noise in my head that almost sounded like howling blocked out anything he might have said.

I wished I had the energy to say something back to him.

To tell him that I wished that I could be that fighter he saw in me. I didn't want to give up. I wanted to have more time. That I would spend it with him. My eyes slid closed against my wishes, and I had no power to open them.

I was just glad that I got a taste of him before I lost myself to the darkness.

AARON

My body thrummed with a disorienting mix of arousal and panic.

Sofia had looked at me, her dazed eyes clearing, as she'd leaned forward and kissed me—I still couldn't believe that she'd kissed me. Then fell back limply to the ground.

"No, Sofia!"

I held her face in my shaking hands as panic raced through my veins. My heartbeat thrashed so hard in my ears that it was all I could hear.

What was happening to her?

My nose could barely detect anything through the overpowering scent of my mate's silver-burned flesh.

I placed my hand against her neck to try to feel for a pulse. To even see if she was still alive. I don't know if I wasn't able to find it because my hand was shaking, or if it was because she was gone.

She was so still. So pale.

I was numb. Unable to feel anything at all as I brushed the back of my hand against the smooth skin of her cheek.

Even lying here, still. Broken. With one arm bent back

at an unnatural angle, Sofia was gorgeous. With all of her quiet and stubborn ferocity at rest, the delicate features of her face were at peace. Lovely.

She looked like she was already gone.

I didn't know why I did it. I was probably too used to getting things that I want. Too stubborn to give up. It had me keep fighting.

"Sofia. Wake up." I lowered my voice into an alpha command. Letting the power of the words flow through me, lacing each word with anger. Anger at the time stolen from her. Anger that my mate would be taken. Death couldn't have her. She was *mine*.

"Don't stop fighting." I intertwined my hand through the limp fingers of her uninjured hand, giving it a squeeze. Praying to the goddess that if she was in there, that she could hear me. "Please."

I swallowed heavily, watching her still form.

Then her broken arm cracked. The sound was as loud as a tree branch snapping in half. Her hand twisted as the bones of her fingers were rearranged. Her thumb shifted up further, and from out of the nails, claws burst out.

Though she didn't seem to be conscious, Sofia was shifting.

I backed up to give her some space, practically holding my breath.

Sofia's back arched off the ground as her bones broke apart and reformed. Her face stretched, skin splitting, as the jaws of the wolf emerged.

Sofia's dress strained at the seams until the silk fabric ripped, revealing her trim abdomen and the underside of full breasts before rough fur covered every inch of her.

Her pelt was black as pitch.

Sofia's wolf shook its fur. Alive and well, despite her ordeal with the silver.

Both my palms hit the ground, and I breathed heavily, panting as if I had run a mile. A tension that I didn't even know I had released in my chest. I felt like I could breathe again. Like I got a reprieve on a prison sentence.

She was alive.

A wet nose prodded at my temple, snuffling and breathing in deeply.

I looked up into the amber eyes of my mate.

I didn't know what I was expecting Sofia's wolf to look like.

I'd heard it said that someone's wolf reveals the inner strength of its human counterpart. There were physically strong people with wolves that came out smaller than terrier dogs; people who were revealed to be cowards.

Sofia's wolf was a beast.

Enormous. Easily the size of a dire wolf—even larger than my own shifted form. All that dark fur over sleek lines of muscle.

She was absolutely gorgeous.

"You're a beauty," I murmured, holding out my hand for Sofia's wolf to sniff.

Her wolf sniffed excitedly at my palm, her tail wagging like a dog. Yipping like a puppy as she began to lick me. Delighted with me.

From within me, my wolf scratched at me, demanding to be let out. He was not oblivious to the clear invitation Sofia's wolf was sending, and he was absolutely panting with the need to get to his mate.

Not yet, I admonished him.

Given the sharp scent of arousal in the air, I couldn't

guarantee that our wolf forms wouldn't hold back from activities that Sofia wasn't emotionally ready for.

Her wolf ran circles around me, crouching in front of me in a bow. Clearly inviting me to play. To transform into my wolf self and go run with her.

Inside me, my wolf whined as he realized that he would not be let out. That he'd have to wait to meet his mate.

After frolicking for some time under the full light of the moon, Sofia's wolf settled down. She lay in a patch of grass in the clearing of the forest and began to shift.

Bones snapped and rearranged; fangs and claws sunk back within her body.

All that gorgeous black fur was replaced by creamy white skin.

With her transformation complete, my mate lay on the grass in front of me. Completely naked and starting to wake.

15

SOFIA

I opened my eyes and instantly realized two things at once.

That I was lying on the forest floor entirely naked.

And two, my mate was standing over me and pulling his shirt over his head.

I parted my lips to protest, to ask him what he was doing, and was struck dumb by the sight of his torso.

He was a towering wall of muscle—chiseled six-pack and broad chest.

My mouth shut as my throat went bone-dry.

Aaron held his shirt out, looking pointedly away from me.

I grabbed his shirt gratefully. Gingerly, I sat up and pulled his shirt over myself. I checked once that he wasn't looking before I sniffed under the collar, taking in the scent of him. It was warm and rich with the scent of cedarwood, bergamot and a hint of something wild. The musk of a predator.

His shirt fell to my upper thigh. I was just glad to not be the one exposed. As I slowly maneuvered myself to get up, pressing against the forest floor on shaky arms, I felt myself suddenly lifted.

Aaron had placed one hand under my knee and the other against my back, carrying me. All of a sudden, I found myself pressed against his bare torso as he cradled me to his chest.

"I can walk." Did he think that I was too weak to get back to the castle?

Aaron shook his head. "Let me take care of you."

Though a part of me wanted to protest that I could take care of myself, a larger part of me was comfortable in those strong arms. I leaned my head against him, huddling into the warmth. The rocking motion of his footfalls were lulling me half to sleep.

I wasn't even aware that he hadn't been walking in the direction of the castle until he stopped at one of the drop offs and put me down. He grabbed a new shirt from the storage bin then turned around, facing away from me. Giving me privacy to change into new clothes.

After rummaging through half the pile of men's sizes, I finally found a pair of pants and underwear that would work and struggled into them. The only pair of shoes in the bin that were remotely my size were at least two sizes too big. I was grappling with the laces—my hands were still quite sore. The skin was too new and raw. Even the material of the laces felt too rough against newly reformed fingers.

I had dropped the laces twice when Aaron placed his large hands over mine, taking over.

"I can tie my shoes by myself," I muttered as he pulled the shoelaces tight and knotted them.

"You almost died," Aaron said in a tone that left room for no argument.

After shutting the drop off bins, he swept me back up

into his arms. I didn't want to be hauled back into the castle like some invalid. But I was also exhausted. Bone-tired.

As the rhythms of his footfalls rocked me, I settled back against him. My protests died somewhere in the warmth of his hold.

"Thank you," I said once we were in view of the castle. I had struggled here alone with my first transformation, feeling the sting of every healed broken bone, all the crude ache of shifting for the first time. I hadn't wanted to make that walk through the forest alone. Not after everything.

I'd thought that he would put me down as soon as I got through the castle doors—he'd avoided the huge gates in the front, and I was happy not to have to ask for him to be discreet. I'd assumed that after that he would put me down. But I was wrong. Aaron continued carrying me through the doors, heading down the corridors at a steady clip.

I stretched out my legs, ready to walk the rest of the way, but Aaron just held me more firmly. Not budging an inch.

"Let me down, people will see us." My eyes flicked up and down the empty hallways, unable to see or scent anyone.

"I'll walk up the servants' path. No one will follow us."

"Servants gossip as well," I scoffed.

"Not about me, they don't. Not if they know what's good for them." His tone was so certain, as if his say so would alter reality. Maybe he was right. That was how things always seemed to work around here. The word of the alpha was law.

I didn't have the energy to argue with him. And if I was really honest with myself, I didn't really have the energy for the long walk up multiple flights of stairs. Not after every-thing that had happened tonight. I let him carry me all the way back up to my room. Aaron set me down on my bed and helped me to take off my shoes. He even pulled the covers out and helped me get into bed.

I felt awful. Exhaustion all the way to the core. And he was so warm.

Maybe I was just tired of the world feeling so cold.

As he turned to head back out, I called out to him. "Could you stay with me?"

16

AARON

All the blood in my body flowed to my cock as Sofia asked me to stay.

I had to get a hold of myself. She probably just wanted someone around to feel safe. It was at the tip of my tongue to tell her that it wasn't a good idea. I wasn't able to control myself around her. That I wasn't sure that I would be able to keep my hands off her.

But I didn't want to stay away from her. Not now. Not ever.

Not when the last time I let her out of my sight, she had almost died.

Sofia's room didn't have any sofa or anything like that for me to crash on. Under her vanity, she had a velvet tufted stool that didn't look remotely capable of holding up my weight. There was just one bed.

I sat on the edge of it. Not wanting to scare her away. Not wanting to be presumptuous.

Sofia stared directly in my eyes, holding my gaze as she pulled back the cover, inviting me in.

I swallowed down the lump in my throat. Without

wasting any time, I pulled off my shoes and joined her in bed. I couldn't resist reaching out to Sofia. Pulling her against my chest and holding her in my arms. She fit so perfectly against me. Like she was made for me.

Sofia sighed, as if she was finally able to relax. She snuggled closer against me. It wasn't long at all before her breaths settled into the deep pattern of sleep.

She was whole again. No longer burned. Shifting had taken away all of the damage. Her neck looked as if nothing had happened to it—delicate and swan-like, with creamy smooth skin.

I wanted to kiss it.

Having Sofia's sleeping form besides me soothed some of the raging anger that still flooded through me. Anger that someone from my own pack wanted to harm her. I never should have come that close to losing her.

A thought nagged at me—why Robert would do this in the first place. It was easy enough to excuse his actions as the pathetic outburst of a jealous slime. Worth less than the growth of mold on week-old bread. But what if it wasn't? What if Robert wasn't working alone?

If Sofia died, the treaty between the Stonevalley and Edgeriver wolves would shatter.

If Sofia died, it would mean war.

In the middle of the night, rustling woke me from a deep sleep. My eyes shot open. I didn't think that I'd be able to fall asleep next to her, that I'd be too keyed up, too stressed. But being so near Sofia was soothing. I must have drifted off.

She was tossing and turning, getting tangled in her sheets. Moaning. Her arms pushed at something that wasn't there. She was having a nightmare.

I grabbed her shoulder and shook her gently. "Hey, Sofia."

Her eyes shot open, wide and filled with terror. She clutched her chest, breathing hard as if she'd been running.

"It's okay." My fingers curled around her shoulder, wanting to pull her in tight against me. I wanted to hold her and chase away all her nightmares. "It's just a bad dream."

She ran her hands through sweat-soaked hair as she exhaled. Tears gathered in the corners of her eyes. Sofia turned to look away from me. "I'm sorry."

"For what?"

"For all of it. For waking you in the middle of night. For dragging you to my room. For needing to be rescued in the first place."

"Hey," I cut her off, giving in to my need to touch her. I pulled Sofia against me. "There isn't anywhere else I'd rather be." I squeezed her tighter in my arms to make my meaning clear. Here. With her in my arms. "And it's not your fault that you were attacked. There isn't a wolf alive who could hold their own any better than you did. Not against silver."

"He's dead now. I should be over it." Sofia shook her head, as if she was frustrated with herself. "Not living through the attack again in my dreams."

Why was my soulmate so hard on herself? After just being assaulted the day before?

"I'm not over it," I admitted to her. The memory of it was burned into my brain, in a fiery rage that still surged close to the surface. "I don't think I've ever been angrier in my entire life than when I saw you hurt. I wish Robert was still alive so I could tear him apart all over again."

Sofia stilled, looking me straight in the eyes. I had no idea what she was thinking until her gaze flicked down to my mouth.

Sofia leaned in closer to me, until our lips were a breath apart. Softly, she closed the distance between us with a kiss.

My entire range of focus was locked into the sweetness of her. The soft pressure as her mouth moved tentatively against mine. I found myself winding my hand through the silky locks of her hair, holding her in place as I kissed her deeper.

As I swept my tongue against hers, Sofia moaned into my mouth.

Heat flooded every inch of me.

My heart pounded as I held her closer. My lips traced a path across her skin. Consumed by her scent. By the soft press of her body against mine.

She was fucking perfect.

The sharp tang of arousal in the air was undeniable. Thick and spicy, the pheromonal message was as clear as if it had been spoken out loud.

Sofia wanted me.

Well, I wasn't in the mood to deny her anything.

17

SOFIA

He broke his lips away from the trail they made across my skin, leaving me keening at the loss of him.

"Do you want me?" His bright blue eyes were heated as they took in my panting, heaving chest.

"Yes." My voice sounded like a moan. Less like a word and more like a desperate plea.

Aaron grabbed my shirt with both hands and tore it open. The fabric parted under his fingers like it was made of soggy paper.

I returned the favor, sliding my fingers under the collar of his shirt. Letting claws burst out of my fingertips, I sliced through. I ran my fingers over the lines of muscles on his back, feeling his warmth. His body was strong. All alpha male. Luxurious. I wanted him closer.

He chuckled his approval in a low rumble, and I could feel the vibrations of it seep into me.

My hands took on a mind of their own as they latched on to the front of his belt, opening it and tugging away at the coarse material separating me from what I wanted.

Aaron grabbed both of my hands in one of his and

pulled them over my head. Stopping me from freeing the part of him I desperately needed.

"Tell me." Aaron nipped along my neck between words. His teeth hit a nerve that sent chills down the entire length of my spine, and I arched my back, pressing against him. "Tell me exactly what you want."

Heat flared in my cheeks and ran up my neck. He was going to make me say it.

"I-I want to feel you. All of you." My voice was high pitched and breathless. I didn't recognize myself. I had turned into a wanton creature, arching my hip against his, desperate for friction. Desperate to soothe that tense coil at the center of me.

Aaron pulled himself up to his knees, and I whimpered at the loss of him.

Slowly—too slowly—he pulled off the rest of his clothes, his eyes locked on mine the entire time. As his cock slipped free from the fabric holding it back, my lips parted. He was thicker than I imagined, with a drop of precum at the tip. Every part of him was strong and perfect.

He was absolutely delicious.

I licked my lips.

His intense blue gaze burned into me as I unbuttoned my pants. Hooking my panties, I drew them down my thighs along with my trousers and kicked them off. Baring myself completely. I could feel the heat of his stare as I opened my thighs wider.

With nothing more than a faint gasp to reveal the effect that I was having on him, Aaron drew closer. Settling himself over me.

He pressed his cock right against my center, and I arched my back, pressing closer. The friction was tantalizing. The first promise of the pleasure we could have together.

"Aaron, please."

"Please what?" His eyes were hooded and locked on mine as he slid his cock in between my wet folds, teasing me with what I wanted. But holding back from what I needed.

"Please." I licked my lips, mentally cursing him for making me say it out loud. "I need you inside of me."

"Are you sure that's what you want?" He was pressing against my clit, and desire curled in me, tight and aching. "Because as soon as I do, everyone's going to know you're mine."

I didn't care if everyone knew. I couldn't take it anymore. I had to have him.

"Please, Aaron. Please fuck me."

The words unleashed something within him. I could see it as his eyes darkened with something wild. Something possessive.

Aaron guided himself to my entrance and pushed into me.

I felt the blunt pressure of him and a brief stab of pain. But more than that, I was drowning in bliss. My walls fluttered around him and he shuddered, grinding his hips against me. In me to the hilt.

He pressed a gentle kiss against my lips and whispered into my ear, "Are you okay?"

In reply, I grasped his face and kissed him back, pouring into the kiss all my desire for him. All the regret that we hadn't done this so much sooner. I stroked my tongue against his, wrapped up in his taste. He felt so unbelievably good.

He broke off the kiss with a moan and grabbed my hip tight as he began to move. Setting a fast pattern, as he rocked within me. I clutched his back, digging my nails into muscles that flexed and tensed. Close enough to hear the thud of his heartbeat, the jagged groans that he couldn't hold back.

"You feel so fucking good." Aaron leaned in and whispered the words into my skin.

Needing him closer, I wrapped my legs around his hips, crossing my ankles just beneath his buttocks. I rocked my body, arching against him as he thrust into me.

Aaron wove his fingers into my hair, holding me in place as he brought his lips to the pulse point at my neck. "You take me so well. That's my good girl."

His praise was like a direct hit to the tension in my core. The taught chord of desire, strung around me tight, ratcheting higher and higher.

"Aaron," I called out. Close to the edge and needing something—something just out of reach.

He reached down between my legs, pressing firmly against my clit.

I shattered beneath him. Breaking apart with nothing but the solid weight of his body holding me together. I fractured into pleasure that rolled through every part of my body in a wave.

I went limp, collapsing flat against the bed. Panting heavily.

Seeing him from behind eyelashes that were heavy, tired out from his love-making—it was like I was looking at someone completely new. Sweat dripping from his golden hair, those perfectly sculpted abdominal muscles flexing and tensing over my body with each delicious thrust. More than anything, that look in his eye as he took me—fierce and claiming.

He was mine.

"I'm close." Aaron trailed his palm along my body, tracing a path from my navel to the peaks of my nipples. "Where would my good girl like me to come? Should I come all over your perfect tits? On that tight little stomach?"

"I want all of you." I met his gaze as I admitted how fully I needed him. "Come inside me."

I watched his eyes dilate and his jaw drop open as my words registered.

It was like he became unhinged.

Aaron pulled my legs over his shoulders and began pounding into me faster, holding me in a bruising grip as he relentlessly sought his pleasure.

With one last sharp thrust, he came, rocking hard and incessantly against me. His cock pulsed in the deepest part of me, coating me in his essence.

He groaned, loud and guttural, stilling. For a moment, Aaron slumped against me, pressing my body deeper into the bed. Every inch of me felt the firm weight of his muscles as he rested on top of me. Catching his breath before finally slipping out of me.

Aaron kissed me. His lips were soft, moving against mine with more tenderness than I thought an alpha like him possessed. With something like devotion.

He stroked up my thighs, gathering up everything that escaped and pushing it back inside me. I couldn't help but whimper as his fingers slipped back into my oversensitive channel.

"I want everyone that comes near you to smell exactly who you belong to," he growled into my ears.

I nodded slowly as his words sunk into me... Who I belonged to.

Not to River wolves, or Stone, but to Aaron.

In all the years I had lived amongst the Stone pack

wolves, I never imagined myself having sex with the heir to their alpha. Being his soulmate.

But here I lay, panting and spent beneath him. Utterly ruined by a man who was supposed to be my enemy.

It was the best fucking thing I'd ever done.

18

AARON

Our scents were wrapped together so perfectly, I could barely tell the two of us apart. Her smell overlaid on top of my skin was an intoxicating combination. I could be happy to live here, in between her thighs. Breathing in the scent of arousal mixed with the smell of my claim on her, pushed deep within her womb. Marking her as mine.

When I closed my eyes, I could recall exactly the look on her face as she shattered beneath me. She was still recovering from her peak. Through the mark of the soulbond, I could feel flickers of it. Her pleasure sang through my blood.

I kissed a path across her shoulders, not quite ready to be separated from her warmth. I stroked the underside of her breast, which I had somehow neglected in my rush to have her. Marveling at the luxurious smoothness of her skin, the gentle give as I pressed against her, stroking my fingers across her pebbled nipple.

Sofia gasped, arching into the contact. Moaning breathlessly. As if she couldn't help it. As if she couldn't resist the pleasure I could bring her.

The sound of her moans went straight to my cock, and I found myself hardening and straining to be inside her again. I leaned down to whisper into the shell of her ear, "I'm not done with you yet."

With my other hand, I reached between her thighs and brushed my fingers against her wet folds, finding that delicate bundle of nerves and massaging against it. Slowly, in gentle patterns, until Sofia's breath began to hitch. She whimpered, bucking her hips against me. Her legs shook as they parted wider for me.

"That's it. That's my girl," I praised her as Sofia's whimpers became higher pitched and somehow grittier, more desperate, as she clenched the sheets tight. I kept up the pressure, right where she needed it, in that same circular rhythm.

Sofia closed her eyes, her head arched back. Her teeth clenched together, so close to the edge. Just needing that little push to fall over.

I deepened my voice to an alpha tone, lacing each word with authority. "Come for me."

Sofia shrieked a garbled cry that sounded like my name.

Capturing her lips with mine, I swallowed her cries with a heated kiss. Taking those impossibly soft lips. Pressing closer. I tangled a hand into the silky locks of her hair, holding her in place as I tasted her deeper.

She was the sweetest thing.

My desire for her was a heat flooding through every inch of my skin, sinking into every pore.

All consuming.

Gazing into the stormy gray of her eyes, now heavily lidded, I told her, "I'm going to fuck you again."

She bit her lip as she nodded.

I didn't break eye contact with her as I slid my cock against the heat of her, pushing until I notched just inside of her. I kept my eyes locked on hers as I thrust hard. Sheathing myself as deep as I could go. Until I had no way to tell where I ended and she began.

Fuck.

She was so tight. Like being enveloped by pure bliss. The velvety pressure all around me was absolutely sublime.

I pulled back, almost all the way out before slamming back into her. Hard.

Hard enough to shift her a few inches up the bed.

Good.

I wanted her sore.

I wanted to make sure Sofia felt me tomorrow. As she walked, as she bent down to lift up her books. I wanted her to feel where I had been and to remember that she was mine.

I started a fast rhythm. Losing myself in the sensation. Intense and coiled. Jolting like electricity every time my balls slapped against her ass. Holding her hips in place tight enough to bruise. Sinking into her over and over again.

Sofia gave as good as she got, digging her nails deep enough into my back to draw blood. The sting of it pleased me. As a sign that my mate had marked me. It was evidence written into my skin of the bond that we shared.

"Oh, goddess," Sofia moaned as she arched her back. Canting her hips. Taking me deeper. The new angle made every single nerve ending light up. Pleasure. Pure and molten. Engulfing me. Chasing after that feeling of bliss, I dug marks like crescent moons onto her skin.

My muscles tensed until the pleasure built up to a fever pitch.

With one last sharp thrust, my cock pulsed deep within her, releasing all the tension in my body as my mind was lost to white-hot bliss.

I collapsed into soft curves, pressing my face into Sofia's shoulder as I struggled to remember how to think.

Sofia mumbled protests, squirming beneath me until I shifted my weight off of her.

I knew I should probably get up. Go into the washroom for something to clean us off. And I would. In just a few minutes I would. But not just yet. I didn't want to break this quiet moment. Lying here in my mate's bed felt unreal. I wanted to bask in this feeling of connection for just a little while longer.

As Sofia lay panting, catching her breath, I gathered her in my arms, tracing patterns against her bare back. She gazed up at me through her eyelashes with a smile that was sleepy and sated.

The thought struck me. Sharp and as jarring as an electric shock. That I came so close to missing out on this moment. This moment and all moments with her. That I came so close to losing her.

She was such a tiny thing. So delicate. Physically, she might be smaller than any of her peers. But I had seen first-hand that every inch of my mate's will power was built with steel.

She was fierce, and lovely. And all mine. Yet someone within the halls of this very castle had tried to kill her.

As my mate drifted back to sleep in my arms, I made her a silent promise. A promise to root out anyone and everyone who had any part of the attack. A promise that I vowed to pay in blood.

19

SOFIA

C lasses were awkward.

There was a wall of silence around me. Without my main tormentor, I was ignored by the others. It was as if I was a ghost in the room, not even really there at all. Which was all I thought I ever wanted. I could actually just focus on my lupine history lesson without a single innuendo or nasty comment. It was almost weird for me not to split my attention on defending myself and shooting back insults.

After the lecture was over, there were strained whispers over classwork. Sharp glances directed at one of the empty chairs in the room. The one where he used to sit.

The others whispered about why he was gone.

"The alpha said that there is an investigation into Robert's disappearance," Evan said in an undertone, after a hasty glance to check that no one around was watching him.

I wasn't looking, not that it mattered. With my wolf senses, I could have been in another room and I would still be able to make out their conversation.

"I heard that the wolves know more about what is going on and are just not saying anything," Mark whispered back.

"Why would they cover that up?"

I put my head down, hunched over my notebook as I worked on my genealogy chart.

I wanted to escape from that night. From the helpless feeling of being held down. Of being powerless while someone who wasn't even one of the wolves decided that I wasn't worthy. That I should pay for my blessing with my life. Robert felt like all of the Stonevalley pack with all his ruthless hatred toward me. The only difference was that he had acted on it.

I'd thought that at least my classes would be a distraction. Instead, I felt a raw vulnerability. Out here, exposed. If one of my classmates decided to try something again, would I be able to take them on? Had I learned from my moment of weakness?

My lupine genealogy chart was half completed, mapping out the royal alpha line and their mates through the past twelve generations.

I felt something drop in the pit of my stomach when I wrote Aaron's name at the bottom of the list. I was confronted with the fact that in the future editions of this text, my name would be on this map. Written out neatly next to Aaron's. That future Stonevalley children would sit here, in this same chair, copying down my name. What would that make me? What would they think of me?

It was as if my own personal history was being wiped away.

"That's a shame that none of us ended up with the wolf gene," Susan whispered. She gave Elise a significant look before tapping on the bottom of their charts.

I didn't need to look at their papers to know that they were talking about Aaron.

My wolf snapped to attention, growling. Attention trained on the pair of them.

"Those alpha types usually end up with their soulmate. But do you think he'd want to play the field before settling down?" Elise pressed her hand over her mouth to stifle a giggle.

Both girls were really pretty, with that athletic build that the guys tended to dream about. Susan had ethereal blonde hair that curled in waves, while Elise had vibrant green eyes under long dark lashes. I had spent years watching the other boys in the class drooling over the pair of them. They were exactly the stuff of every guy's fantasy, and they knew it. The two of them had made it clear to me exactly where I fell in the social hierarchy. How my level of attraction ranked in comparison to theirs.

My wolf huffed in her version of a scoff. As far as she was concerned, her mate only had eyes for one other. He wouldn't give a shit if either of those two came crawling over his way.

I wondered what they would think if they knew that Aaron's soulmate was currently three seats behind them, listening in to their conversation, with his cum slowly dripping out into her panties?

I hung back as class ended, waiting for the rest of my cohort to leave. I pretended to be thinking about what to write. Putting embellishments on the paper that really didn't need to be there as I stared at Aaron's name at the bottom of the genealogy chart. Hanging back until I was completely alone in the room.

I sighed, brushing away the strand of hair that fell in front of my face, wishing that I could brush away the dark thoughts swirling away underneath. Thoughts spiraling out of control in my mind.

Finally, I packed all my books together, hustling to get out of the room before I was late to my next lesson. I had to get my shit together. Nothing that went on in class ever phased me before. Why couldn't I get a grip on myself?

A warm hand grabbed my arm as I walked down the hall. Pulling me down an otherwise abandoned corridor. After the attack, the sudden pressure binding my hand, restricting my movement, would have scared me. That was, if I hadn't immediately recognized his scent. A scent that had heat pooling in my belly. A scent that had my wolf perking up and preening.

Prickly cedarwood and sunny bergamot. The smell of my mate.

Aaron pulled me down the hallway, in the opposite direction from my next classroom. I toyed with the idea of putting a stop to this. To remind him of my schedule and my academic commitments. How it was important to me to finish my studies with high grades. But I didn't want to lie to him. Or to myself.

I knew exactly why he was here.

And I wanted this.

Aaron pulled me into an empty room. Inside, the smells of people were faded. No one had used this area for a week at least and possibly more. As soon as the two of us were inside the classroom, Aaron closed the door shut and firmly locked it.

In the next moment his lips were on mine. I opened my mouth, taking him in fully.

Heated scorching pleasure laced through every inch of me, pooling straight in my core. Everything about him—the roughness of his hands, his smell, the possessive way he clutched me in his arms. He just felt so fucking good.

Aaron backed me against the wall; one large hand held

both of mine firmly in place above my head. His free hand began to tease me, slipping in underneath my shirt and ghosting over my stomach, tracing a path over the sensitive peaks of my breasts.

Every move that he made felt fucking fantastic.

I squirmed in his hold. My arms tugging, testing his iron grip, needing to break free and trace all the firm lines and textures of his body.

He broke away from the heated path that he was kissing across my neck. "What's wrong?"

"What?" My head was spinning. Desire was flooding me, overriding my capacity for reason. What was he talking about?

"You're tense," he murmured, skimming his rough fingers lightly across my back. "And I can smell the anxiety coming off of you in waves. What's going on?"

I pressed my lips shut in a tight line. Not wanting to admit it. All right. So maybe I was feeling anxious about Susan and Elise's conversation. But it wasn't like it was something that Aaron and I had ever discussed. I never had to think about it before.

Aaron scooped me up in his arms, carrying me away from the wall. He placed me down on the top of a desk, then proceeded to rub up and down my thighs in soothing patterns.

"Hey." He took my chin in his large hand, forcing me to meet the intense look in his blue eyes. "You can tell me."

His look was patient. Patient and unrelenting.

I could read the fierce stubbornness in the firm set of his jaw. He wouldn't be the one to give in.

I sighed. "It was nothing. Just something stupid someone said in class."

Aaron shook his head slowly. "It's not stupid if it's making you upset."

His stare was the fixed and absolute attention of a predator. He was really going to make me say it.

"It was just... that your name came up in class."

"Did it?" Aaron raised an eyebrow. "And that made you nervous?"

I shook my head, not wanting him to get the wrong impression.

"Well, it was the alpha genealogy line. Some girls were wondering who you'd end up with. Whether you would sleep around before settling down."

I flushed deep red across my cheeks. I couldn't believe I actually said that out loud. I had most definitely not meant to say that out loud. Damn it.

He smiled a crooked smile as his hands resumed tracing paths along my body. Running up my thighs, pushing up the hem of my dress. Revealing all the hidden parts of myself to him. "I must not be making you come enough if you think I'm interested in anyone other than you."

My mouth dropped open, and Aaron smirked as his hands gripped my thighs and firmly pushed them apart. He knelt on the ground before me, so that his head was about level with my hips.

"Maybe this will convince you." His voice was deep, and so close I could feel the vibrations at my core. I could feel his breath on my inner thighs.

All at once, Aaron pulled my panties to the side. One long, hot swipe of his tongue swept across my pussy.

I arched my head back as a high-pitched shriek was ripped out of me.

Holy goddess. Fuck.

I pressed my palm over my mouth to stifle the rest of my

cries, only to have that hand ripped away. Aaron broke away from his gentle sucking pressure. Right where I needed him. "Don't. I want to hear you."

As I slowly placed my hand down to my side, Aaron went back to his work, sinking his hot tongue into the depths of my folds. Unerringly finding my clit. Working me with a flicking pressure.

I was clenching on nothing, feeling empty. Needing more. Needing him. As if Aaron could hear the desperate thoughts swirling around in my head, he plunged one finger into my dripping center.

I gasped, bucking my hips. Trying to seek him out, to get closer against him. Both my hands wove between the golden locks of his hair, holding him closer as he devoured me.

My clenched teeth were all that were in the way of my broken moans slipping from my lips. I didn't want anyone to hear. But more than that, I didn't want to hold back my cries and have Aaron make good on his threat to stop.

The friction, the perfect wet glide of him on my throbbing clit, the press of his fingers within me—it all worked me into a perfect storm. Pushing me higher. Coiling me up and winding me tight until there was nothing left of me but that molten vibrating tension.

Aaron pulled my clit directly into his mouth, sucking hard, just as his fingers speared into me tight, hitting something deep within me.

With a high-pitched whimper, I broke—my walls clenching and gripping his finger within me. Grasping tight on the back of his head, as if it was all I had to hold all of me together. I was flooded with pulsing waves of bliss that rolled through each and every one of my limbs. Pleasure tumbled through every inch of me.

As I shuddered, trying to regain my breath, Aaron

straightened. He tugged off his belt and opened up his pants, freeing himself.

I watched the zipper of his pants pull down with hooded eyes until his cock sprung free—thick and glorious.

I licked my lips, not able to help myself.

"You got me so fucking hard, I'm not going to last long," Aaron warned me as he lined himself up against me.

With one strong thrust, he pushed all the way into me. Hard enough to tip the desk back.

I wrapped my arms against his neck as I squealed, gripping down on his back.

"Shit," Aaron murmured.

He pressed hard against me, circling around, in me to the hilt. Grasping my hips tightly. Like he needed me too. Holding me like I was the only thing rooting him to the world.

Aaron started a brutal pace, working me hard. Slamming into me relentlessly.

I felt his power, coiled through each of his shifting muscles. Through his possessive grip, cleaving me to him. In the delicious friction of him moving within me. Through the hot look in his eyes that didn't break away from me as he took me.

With one last, harsh thrust, he drove in deep. Until I could feel the warm pressure of his sculpted torso against my body. Until I could feel him throbbing against my cervix.

He groaned, low and strained against my ear, before he stilled. His forehead rested against my shoulder, and his hard body slumped against mine.

When he recovered, he pressed a sweet kiss against my lips. Cupping my cheek against his hand. Like I was delicate. Like I was precious to him.

"Hey." His blue eyes were fierce and piercing as they gazed into mine. "I've never been with anyone else. I never want to be with anyone else. Those girls can go fuck themselves because I won't be fucking them."

Oh.

I hadn't known that he hadn't done it before.

Now that I thought about it, Aaron was the kind of traditional alpha-type who would wait for their mate. There was a whole issue of dominance. Sex was seen as favor, and impacted ranking in the pack.

But the alphas weren't the only ones. Many wolves, especially in the Stonevalley pack, held off on relationships, or treated their partners casually as they sought out their soulbond. It was even common for the younger pack members to hold off on dating until they came of age—in case they ended up as a wolf with their own soulmate.

It wasn't that I'd ever seen Aaron with anyone else. I'd just never asked. Honestly, there was one main reason why I was surprised that he hadn't had any experience. Aaron did not fuck me like a virgin.

He was still watching me with heat in his eyes.

What could I say to that?

"You were really good. I never would have guessed that your first time was with me." I found myself blushing again. It was something I never thought that I'd say to him out loud. But Aaron had a way about him of making me feel like it was all right to say things I'd never admit to anyone. Something about him was raw, almost feral and unapologetically himself. That freed things within me that I always thought would have to be locked inside.

"Guys talk. I listened." Aaron shrugged. Nonchalantly. As if skipping the fumbling awkward virgin phase was just a part of being an alpha wolf. Maybe it was. Maybe anything as natural and primal as sex would come easily to someone as dominant as him. His eyes darkened as he pressed his forehead against mine. Close. Inhaling deeply as if he wanted to breathe me in. "I haven't even scratched the surface with the things I want to do to you."

His words shuddered through me. Awakening in me a hunger I didn't even know I was capable of.

I pulled his face to mine and kissed him. Showing him with my body all the things that I was afraid to show the world in the light of day. That I wanted him. That I didn't care that he was born from a bloodline that warred against my people. His lineage, his status, none of that mattered to me. Just the man he was underneath.

I could feel it now; we were a matching pair. Connected by more than our souls. More than the marks etched across us.

Something raw and savage lived just beneath his skin. A wildness that rivaled my own.

I didn't have a place back at my birth home anymore, and I would never truly belong here in the land of my enemies, either.

But I belonged with Aaron.

20

AARON

I made a show of carefully grasping the teacup and taking a measured sip from it. Noticing the delicate floral flavors and spices in case Mother asked me about any of it.

This was the second time I'd been called to her quarters this month. The last time, barring a few purely social visits, was three months ago.

Could this mean that she had a message to send me from the alpha?

If the alpha was displeased with my work, he could send me an order that I would not be able to refuse. An order that would force me to choose between Sofia and my responsibilities. Impacting my availability to protect her. I had to avoid that at all costs.

I looked at the decorations in her room, at the dark oak furniture. The tufted velvets and the wall hangings depicting famous battles with our ancestors. If I had paid attention to any of it before, I would know what to point out. I would be able to compliment her decorative tastes. It could soften the blow. Have her reevaluate and take the conversation back to the alpha.

I placed the teacup firmly back down on the lacquered tray and stared resolutely at Mother. She was making a show of carefully adding milk and sugar into her tiny porcelain cup. Placing each item back on the tray with dainty care. This whole process was tedious.

Mother sipped from her teacup, staring decisively at a floral arrangement at her table. As if the two of us had all of the time in the world. Clearly waiting for me to break the silence.

Her movements had a hint of stiffness to them. An extra layer of precision. She had also masked her scent with her vanilla and clove perfume, strong enough that I couldn't get a read on her emotions at all.

Well, it gave me a chance to direct the conversation. I took a stab at talking about Sofia.

"I worked things out with my soulmate."

"I know. I can smell her on you." Mother swirled her spoon within her tea, gently tapping the sides of the glass.

Something about her tone put me on alert.

Mother's eyes narrowed as she stared into her tea. Her lips were pursed, as if I had mentioned something obscene.

Was she annoyed that I had claimed Sofia? She was my soulmate. What else did Mother expect me to do?

"You don't still consider her my sister, do you?" I said each word with care. How could her status as a member of our family be a problem? Sofia wasn't genetically related to me. I had never considered her as my true sister, and I wasn't going to start now. Not now when she was more. Now that I knew her. Now that every fiber of me burned with the ache to get closer to her. That itched with an anxious desire to protect her whenever she wasn't around.

"Are you sure that you want to do this?" Mother fixed me with a piercing look. One that seemed to pick me apart, break me down and scrutinize every inch of me. "If you didn't want to, you haven't publicly accepted her. You could still call things off."

I had to force myself to take a measured breath as, beneath the table, claws burst through my fingertips. "Did you invite me here to tell me to break things off with my mate?" I said quietly.

Was I reading this wrong? Or was it true? Did Mother really want me to reject Sofia?

If that was true. What the fuck?

What the hell was she saying? This was coming from the woman who raised me to wait for my soulmate.

Mother cleared her throat delicately, interrupting my spiraling thoughts. "Then you have chosen her?"

"She's my mate. She was chosen for me by the goddess." I hadn't publicly claimed her, but I would when she was ready.

What the hell was Mother getting at?

Mother placed her teacup down, a frown marring her aristocratic features. "I don't know how I am going to tell your father about this."

I banished wishful thoughts of hurling the pitcher, the cups and tray against the wall. Breaking Mother's prized glassware wouldn't win me any favors.

"Just tell him. I'm sure that he would be more under-standing," I muttered, half under my breath. Or if he wasn't, that was something that I needed to know.

"I told you before that this isn't what your father and I wanted for you," Mother began with a sigh.

"Then what do you expect of me? Do you really think that I would abandon my mate? I've been waiting my whole life to meet her." I couldn't stomach the malice in her voice. Not when it was directed toward Sofia. Sofia, who already had the whole of the castle against her. Sofia, who had accepted me in spite of everything.

"Your whole life," Mother scoffed. "You are barely in your twenties, and you want to tie yourself down to the River wolf? When you could have anybody?"

Rage, pure and red-hot, was pulsing through every inch of my body. I was practically vibrating as adrenaline charged through my veins.

I brought both hands under the table as I clenched them into a fist hard enough for blood to seep from my palms; my wolf nails pierced directly though my flesh. A trickle of blood dripped through my tight fist to puddle down on Mother's priceless Turkish cotton rug.

So much for making a favorable impression.

I was done with formalities. I had to get out of here before I did something that I would come to regret. I shifted to get to my feet. "Just tell me what the alpha called me for and then let me get on my way."

I couldn't help but think back to my last conversation with Mother. How she was offering a betrothal party. Custom made jewelry. My girl deserved all those things. She deserved recognition for that hidden well of strength within her. For all her bravery. For everything that she was.

My mate deserved the entire fucking world, and it looked like my parents wanted to deprive her from all of it. None of this was fucking fair.

"Oh, sit down," Mother said, irritation coloring every word. "The alpha asked me to discuss the Robert situation with you."

I could barely hear her over the pounding of anger thrumming through my veins.

I stared hard at a painting, not focusing on the vivid

colors of it. Instead reaching out, seeking out my mate's presence. Breathing deeply, straining my hearing.

She was supposed to be in her biologics and astrology class right now. The colors around the room began to fade, some hues slipping into gray as I stretched my senses out. Checking on her. All the noises in the class blended together somewhat. It wasn't a perfect system. But there was a relative quiet in her classroom. No sounds of struggles. No obvious taunting.

I released my hold on my wolf senses, letting the colors snap back into focus. Just as my mother sighed heavily as if *I* were the one who was being ridiculous. She reached into her drawer, pulling out a glass vial. The three drops that she poured into her drink were sharp and sickly sweet. It had the cloying scent of painkillers. I couldn't quite tell under the stench of strong vanilla and clove, but I hadn't noticed any endorphins signaling pain in her body recently.

Her movements were quick and impatient now as she downed her tea, chugging it all down in one go.

"The Ingolfs naturally have questions about the treatment of their son. Understandable, as he was the last of their line."

"You read my report?" I trained my attention on the movement of her hands as they relaxed. Loosening their hold on the teacup handle.

"I did."

"So you know that he broke into the armory, stole silver and then used it to try to kill my mate?"

"Aaron, you ripped his head off." Mother's gaze was piercing, as if I was a child caught in the middle of an act of disobedience. "He was the last of a very prestigious line."

"What are you suggesting? That I should have let him kill her? That I should have turned a blind eye because of his lineage?" I couldn't help but to raise my voice. "Do you really think that I would sit back and watch him use silver to destroy a wolf in our pack? If he can turn against my mate, he can come after any of us. If he was standing here right now, I would kill him all over again."

"That's not how the others will see it." Mother shook her head. "You ended a bloodline. You have to know how people are going to interpret that. We don't have enough wolves left to dole out that kind of justice."

"You are forgetting what would have happened if that piece of shit succeeded in killing my mate. It would have meant war. How many have we lost fighting against the River wolves? How many deaths should we put at stake all to protect the rebellious backside of Robert Ingolf the third?"

"Aaron. I say this as your mother." She looked at me with a long-suffering look on her face. "You are more than just my son. You are destined to be the next alpha. To lead the next generation of Stonevalley wolves. If you want the respect of your pack, you need to watch what you say about that girl. If the people believe that she is behind the scenes pulling the strings, no one is going to take that sitting down. Alphas have been overthrown in the past. I couldn't bear to see my son face the end of our dynasty, all for some scrap of a girl. Not when there's still time to do something about it."

I got to my feet. The abrupt motion jostled the tray and nearly toppled over the entire set of delicate drinks.

"My relationship is not up for discussion."

"Aaron..." Mother began.

I cut her off with one cold look.

If separation was the path she would choose for me, Mother's opinion didn't matter.

I wanted to be with Sofia. There wasn't another option on the table.

I had already experienced what it was like to lose her. What it was like to watch her torn away from me. She had been so close to dying, and it had ripped me apart. The worst pain I had ever experienced.

"I'm done."

If Mother was asking me to choose between Sofia and anything else... Well, then I didn't have a choice at all, then.

I would always choose her.

21

SOFIA

I hadn't really thought about Aaron's comment that once we started sleeping together, everyone would know it. My classmates treated me exactly the same. But then again, none of my classmates were wolves.

I had always been aware of the Stone wolves. They were the ones who could barely control their reactions to me. Always on the cusp of violence around me for all the years that I had lived within these castle walls. They were the ones with a curled lip, with a hint of fang. The ones with hands that would glint with the cruel edges of claws when I drew near. I had learned to stay away from them.

Now that I was supposed to be one of them, I still stayed away. It wasn't that I didn't trust Aaron. I knew that he would do everything in his power to keep me safe. But he hadn't lived within the walls of this castle in my skin, watching the hate linger in their expressions. The eyes of predators watched me out of human faces. I had not unlearned the caution developed through my time here.

As I was walking down the hallway, I had developed the habit of tucking my head in and stretching out my wolf senses as I walked. Waiting for the halls to clear of noise. I thought that it was a good system until I walked straight into someone's back. I was focused out too far and was blind to what was right in front of me. Even before he whirled around a snarl etched across his features, ready to lay into me, I knew that I had screwed up.

I had walked straight into General Albertsen. His face might still look youthful, with the faintest hint of scars that slashed across his eyebrows and throat, but he was one of the older wolves. I had seen his name in my lupine history class as one of the soldiers who had fought battles over a hundred and fifty years ago.

Against my people.

Decades of muscle memory came to the surface as he grabbed my arm in a crushing grip, pulling me closer. I winced, bracing myself for the blow, tensing every one of my muscles against the attack. The slash.

But it never came.

The General cocked his head, like I was some prey animal and he was considering the best way to rip me apart. The glare in his eyes shuttered as he leaned in closer to me. His jaw tightening as his nostrils flared. Taking in my scent.

Was Aaron right? Could the wolves smell him on me?

If nobody knew about my soulmark, what would Aaron's scent on me mean? He was the heir to the alpha. The second highest-ranking wolf in the entire pack. And me? I was the River wolf that they did their best to ignore.

The General released my arm like it had burned him. Eyes narrowed, like he had never seen me before. He turned, walking in a completely different direction than he had come from. That was nothing like any other reaction I'd ever gotten from one of the wolves. If anything, turning and retreating was the kind of reaction I would expect to see if someone had disrespected the alpha in some way.

But what exactly did he scent on me? Could he tell that I had been sleeping with Aaron? Or did he also know that I was a wolf?

More importantly, what was he going to do with that information?

I might not be able to keep my secret for long. But I wanted to hold on to any anonymity I could, for as long as I could. Until recently, it was all I could trust to keep me safe.

I held my usual sage green dress in the light, examining the faint stain from different angles. The worst of it was gone, but the dress was still obviously discolored, right in the front and center. There were ways to disguise the damage. I could throw a shawl on and drape it over the front. I ran my finger over the delicate silk. I would never be able to wear it again without remembering exactly the kind of disrespect shown to me in it. I could still smell traces of the wine within the material, and it brought to mind everything. Kara's hidden smirk. Her subtle taunting. The underlying message she sent was clear. No matter what I wore, or how many classes I took, I would never be one of the Stonevalley wolves.

Which was fine. I didn't belong here, and I knew that.

I placed my sage silk dress deep into the back of my closet, likely never to take it out again, and pulled out a few possible replacements for it. There was the yellow lace ensemble I had gotten years ago that looked childish on me. A velvet dress that was all wrong for my figure. I sifted through several day dresses more suitable for everyday wear than for formal dinner attire.

Reaching all the way in the back of the closet, I considered a dress that I had never worn before. A chiffon ball gown. Though I liked the dress, I'd avoided it. The A-line construction in the front and the high slit up the side were too flashy.

There was also a modest cashmere number in a dove gray. It was plain, yet well-constructed. A dress that would help me fade into the background and avoid scrutiny. It was exactly the sort of outfit I was looking for tonight.

But I couldn't look away from the chiffon gown. Sliding my fingers over the buttery smooth material, I realized that the color of the dress was an almost exact match for Aaron's eyes.

I could almost picture the expression of his face as he peeled it off of me.

Without giving myself time to talk myself out of it, I stepped into the chiffon ball gown, drew up the zipper, and smoothed down invisible wrinkles from the front of it.

The dress felt sophisticated. Wearing it, I looked and felt like the kind of woman that would make the others think twice before splashing with wine. Completing the look with silk gloves and pearls, I headed over to the dining hall before I could lose my nerve.

As soon as I stepped through the doorway, my heart dropped into the pit of my stomach as all of my skin began to itch.

People were staring at me.

Blood rushed through my limbs as every thought in my head was reduced with the need to run.

What the hell was I doing? This wasn't something that I

did. This went against every single decision I had made in the past half-decade to keep myself safe.

My cheeks burned red as too many eyes lingered on me. What was worse, the table of lesser nobles that usually tolerated my presence was full. I couldn't sneak over to a new table with all the attention that this form-fitting dress was bringing down on me. Could I slip away back to my room after so many people had already gotten a glimpse of me?

The hard slide of a chair being pulled back jolted me out of my thoughts. My gaze jerked to the source of the sound, almost involuntarily, and my eyes locked on Aaron's. He had pulled out the chair next to him at the high table, and he kept his eyes fixed on me.

I gulped.

Everyone watching would know that Aaron had signaled me over. It didn't leave me with any choice.

I lifted my chin as I headed over to Aaron. Aaron, who was sitting at the top of the high-table. Near the alpha and all of the high-ranking nobles. I walked at a measured pace. Steady. Running always set off predators, putting them on the offensive. At least outwardly I was calm, though I wanted nothing better than to high tail it and run back to my room like the biggest coward who lived in these stone walls.

I sat down next to Aaron, attempting to look normal. Casual. Even though I wanted nothing more than to melt down into the seat and disappear.

If looks could kill, the glares sent my way would have left me bleeding out all over the seat cushions. Down the table, Kara held her fork in a white-knuckle grip as if she wanted to hurl it straight at me.

Under the table linen, Aaron's large hand slipped under

the high slit of my dress to grasp my thigh. Squeezing me reassuringly.

The warmth of his touch did more than distract me from my worries.

"Careful," Aaron murmured quietly—a warning about all the pheromones in the air.

I took a steady breath as he slipped his fingers further up my thighs, close to my core.

I closed my eyes, trying to shut out the lust churning through me.

Damn him.

My throat went absolutely dry. Fuck. Just one simple touch of his hands had me wanting him all over again. How was I going to protect my anonymity when all I wanted to do was turn in my chair and let Aaron stick his tongue down my throat?

I straightened my body posture and began to pay attention to the meal. Hoping that something on the menu would make me hungry for something else.

The first course was a soup with hearty broth, filled with root vegetables, with the clean and earthy taste of parsley paired with salty bits of bacon. I took small bites, determined to focus on my meal.

Fuck. Aaron was stroking patterns along the inside of my thigh.

It hadn't been that long since the last time we were alone together. Most nights, he slept in my bed. I'd never slept better in my life than I did wrapped around him. But he had some pack business that took him away last night.

Really. Two days shouldn't feel like it was so long.

I bit the inside of my cheek hard enough to draw blood, forcing my attention away from the soft caresses that felt so damn good. I tuned in to the conversations around the high table.

The conversation was stilted all around us. The alpha's mate was staring pointedly away from us. How many of the other wolves had guessed what I was? If they hadn't, when would they?

The thought crossed my mind that the highest concentration of wolves sat at the high table. While I was sitting next to Aaron, would the others be able to tell that I smelled like him? Would the proximity and the attention he was paying me just end up causing more suspicion?

How long did I have left before everyone knew what I was? What would happen when people learned the truth?

What kind of violence would that open against me?

22

AARON

Too many Goddamn eyes were on my mate. Within my body, my wolf was raging, demanding to break free and spill enough blood that none of the others would ever dare to even look at what was mine. Because if anything was sure to improve Mother's opinion of my mate, mass bloodshed was *sure* to be the thing to do it.

It didn't help that Sofia looked absolutely stunning. Unlike the other pack members, she typically dressed in a reserved fashion. Her clothing was pretty modest compared to the elaborate getups of other nobles.

Not tonight. Tonight, she was showing off all her lush body.

Though small and lithe, she was all feminine—made of delicious curves in a lovely hourglass figure. Generous hips and perky breasts. There was nothing I loved more than the soft give of her flesh, especially when it was pressed under me. As she gave everything to me.

But now other males in the room were staring openly at what was mine. Curiously eyeing the gorgeous form that

Sofia normally kept hidden away. As if she was any old unclaimed female that they could fuck with.

I wanted to pluck their eyes out.

My rational side could reason that I hadn't made my claim on her public. That other men could look at her all they wanted, and it would never mean anything. It was only a matter of time before Sofia would realize the truth. That she could never hide what she was. That a wolf as powerful as her was never made to hide in the dark.

As soon as she said the word, I'd make our relationship public. Once I did, the others would back the fuck off. None of them would even dare to look at her in such a disrespectful manner in front of me.

But human rationality was not enough to cool that wild feral violence rising in my beast.

My vision was clouded in a haze of red as my wolf raged within me. Their stares were intolerable. I wanted to bend her over the table in front of all of them and show them that she was not theirs.

My mate hid a savage beast within her, and none of these other males would ever be worthy of her.

I called her over, scraping the chair next to me out for her to sit on. Meeting her gaze as I did it, daring her to sit somewhere else. If she tried it, I was going to lose my damn mind.

She would never belong to any of them.

Their fucking eyes better mind their own business.

As soon as I had her next to me, the wolf checked her scent. Once he was satisfied that she'd not been harmed, he settled down enough that I could think again.

Goddess above, she was gorgeous. Her blue gown hugged her figure. Cut low enough to tease at all the gifts underneath. With a slit up the side revealing a glimpse of the firm muscles of her legs. Legs that I intended to have around me as soon it was possible for me to get away from this dinner.

Once I was myself enough to get my head out of the pheromonal haze of lust and wolf rage, I realized that Sofia was nervous.

Why was my girl nervous?

The last time she was here, my cousin tossed a glass of wine at her, but she had to know that no one would be stupid enough to try that. Not with me right next to her.

I could give her something else to think about.

The skin of her thighs was softer than the finest silk. Tracing patterns against her buttery smooth leg, my mind wandered to later on in the night. Letting her know with gentle brushes and light touches exactly what I wanted to do to her. There was no way I was going another day without the feel of her legs wrapped around me.

Sofia breathed in deeply, closing her eyes.

The sharp spike of her arousal floated into the air. Sweet and spicy and intense enough that every wolf at the table would pick up on it soon enough.

"Careful," I warned her in a low voice.

Though, truly, being careful was the furthest thing from my mind. There was nothing better than seeing Sofia lose herself to her pleasure. My hand slipped deeper up her thigh.

Was she wet for me? Could I have her soaking for me in front of everyone, with most of the castle none the wiser? What would my girl give in to? Her need for anonymity, or her need for pleasure? Would she take that risk? With the noble wolves and high-ranking generals all around us, the perfume of my mate's arousal was just barely obscured by the smells of spices and seasoning.

Sofia straightened, and all at once the smell of her arousal faded. She tucked into her meal, savoring the first course with rapt attention.

Inside my own head, I smiled, keeping my face blank. So that was how she wanted to play it. Well, lucky for her, I was up for the challenge.

Without giving away what I was doing with something obvious—shifting my position, leaning closer, or anything like that—I carefully brushed my thumb closer to her inner thigh. Stroking the exact pattern that I would apply to her clit later in the night.

Sofia kept her poker face, simply starting on her second course. Tonight, it was crispy pork. She ate it with delicate precision. Though my stroking fingers were close enough to her core that I could practically feel the heat of her. Almost close enough to plunge a finger into the wetness soaking through the thin strip of fabric that was the only barricade between us.

Mother was glaring at the two of us—when she wasn't looking pointedly away from us, pretending that Sofia didn't exist. I doubted that she was close enough to be able to tell what my hands were doing. Here at the dinner table, surrounded by polite company. No, that wasn't the reason for her disapproval.

This was a dangerous game we were playing. Toeing the line between hiding our relationship and revealing it to everyone in the castle.

In Mother's eyes, sitting next to Sofia was crossing a line. Breaking a barrier that could not be unbroken. Again, that was all fine with me. I wasn't going to give her up.

As soon as it was socially acceptable to leave, Sofia shifted impatiently and I let go of her, letting her slip away from the dining hall.

I doubt Sofia had any idea of how gorgeous she looked. How, behind her back, heads turned. The men stared at her with dazed expressions. Even one of the girls in her cohort eyed Sofia with a scowl.

Her dress cascaded around her shapely legs, flowing about her like water. I listened to the soft tread of her ballet flat shoes as she walked at a steady clip out of the hallway and back up to her room. I strained my hearing, listening to make sure that no one got close to her. I wouldn't be able to get away until more of the nobels left, even though I was dying to follow her now.

"Aaron," Mother called me softly, still not looking at me.

The hand under the table that had just caressed my mate tensed into a fist. This had better not be another thing about Sofia.

"Have you spoken with Tora, the eldest daughter of the house of Hansen?" Mother was cutting up her fourth course into smaller pieces without eating any of it. Simply mangling the delicate pastry and berries into bits on her plate.

What?

My eyes flicked over to the girl in question. She was blonde, fit and conventionally attractive. From a good family. The Hansens produced a fair number of wolves throughout the generations. Though, in recent years, many of the generals had been lost in battles, and their numbers had dwindled substantially.

She was a wolf. One of the last ones chosen by the Moon goddess, maybe three or four years before me. We weren't close enough that our class schedules ever over-lapped. Obviously, I had seen her around the castle. We never had much of a reason to speak with one another. She was never mentioned in any of the alpha reports.

"No, not recently." What was Mother getting at?

"She's a wolf similar in age to you." Her eyes were fixed on her plate. Finding more and more pastry to cut up. Her dessert was starting to look mashed into bits, and I still had no idea what her point was. Mother finally set her fork and knife down at the table to meet my gaze. "It would be a politically advantageous match."

What. The. Actual. Fuck.

Was Mother actually trying to set me up with someone else? Right after I told her last week that I wasn't interested? Why did Mother have such an issue with my soulmate? Though unexpected, Sofia was the one who the goddess had chosen for me.

My appetite completely soured. I was done here. Sick of having the same argument over again. Traditionally, it was expected for me to stick around the dining hall. Easy access in case any of the wolves had anything to report, or if any of the human members of the Stonevalley pack had any issues or concerns to bring up to their leaders. It was a task that I had taken on more heavily in the last year. The alpha wanted to ensure that his heir had the proper experience.

I had to get the fuck out.

Throwing my napkin on to my plate, I abandoned my seat at dinner. Let Mother complain to the alpha that I wasn't doing my due diligence. It was better than if she had reported that I had broken down at dinner and caused a scene with his mate.

Halfway down the hallway, the scent of vanilla and clove drifted my way, stopping me as effectively as if she had shouted out my name. I turned to face her.

Both of Mother's hands were clenched tight at her side, and some strands of hair escaped from her elaborate updo, making her look a little wild.

"I can't believe that I have to say this to you. Aaron, you are not thinking about what is best for your people. I can't believe that a son of mine is thinking with his cock."

I couldn't do anything other than stare at Mother. I thought that my mouth hung open.

She took my silence as an invitation to say more. "Aaron, you need to start thinking about what is right for your people. This isn't like you."

I shook my head at her. I couldn't talk to Mother right now. Not when I didn't know whether I'd be able to hold back from saying something that I would regret. I didn't have the emotional space to deal with this. Like I had told Mother before, my relationship wasn't up for discussion.

But I had the feeling that Mother wasn't finished with me.

I never expected that the woman who had given me life and raised me to believe in the blessing of the moon goddess would be the one seeking to rip my soulmate out of the picture.

23

SOFIA

The soft knock came at my bedroom door earlier than I expected. I had barely gotten back to my room, and Aaron usually stuck around the hall for a while after eating. He shouldn't have been back yet.

I hesitated for a moment, then scowled at myself.

Why was I letting myself live in fear? As if I was going to get assaulted again at any moment. My attacker was gone. Decapitated. Buried in the ground. I was acting like a mouse, not a wolf.

I braced myself for whoever it could be, my mind racing for potential confrontations. Could it be a member of the Ingolf family that found out more information and came to take their revenge out on me? Was it General Albertsen here to question me about the nature of my relationship with the heir to the alpha?

I unlocked the door and found Aaron at the other side of it. Though he looked tense. His jaw was clenched tight, and I could smell traces of his blood in the palms of his hands. I stepped to the side to let him in, latching the door firmly shut behind him.

Before I could even turn around, Aaron grabbed me firmly by my hips and leaned down to press hot, open-mouthed kisses down my neck. I could feel myself relaxing in his hold. All the tension, all the worry, was melting away.

Aaron pulled his lips away from my neck. "Are you mad at me?"

What?

I was about to be if he didn't get back to kissing me.

"For what?" I wanted to lean back into him. Let the fiery heat of his kisses make me forget everything. Until nothing existed but the warmth of his hands.

"For seating you next to me."

The reminder cooled some of the heat flowing through the blood in my veins. I looked over my shoulder into his hooded gaze. "Why did you?"

He had demanded my presence in front of everyone. It wasn't quite claiming, but it would raise suspicion.

The rest of the wolves would figure out what we were to each other soon, if they had not already. But I still wanted to keep Aaron all to myself for now. While it was still possible to keep our connection quiet.

"Other men were looking at you."

I stared at him blankly. Of course they were looking at me. I was a River wolf. Their blood enemy, strolling into dinner. I was a wolf in sheep's clothing.

His grip on me tightened. "If I had to spend another minute in there, watching one more man undress you with his unworthy eyes, I was about to lose control and start a bloodbath."

"What are you talking about?"

"You have no idea. Absolutely no idea how gorgeous you are. What you do to me." He pressed against me so that I could feel the hardness of him growing against me.

"I wore it for you," I admitted to him.

Aaron brushed his rough hands over the silky chiffon, caressing my chest through the thin fabric. His deft fingers brushed against my nipples until they hardened into peaks as he ground his cock against my ass. Letting me feel how hard he was for me, the full extent of his desire. He unzipped my dress, drawing the silky fabric away from my shoulders, kissing the exposed skin.

"This is all for me?" he repeated, sliding his hands down my body, pulling the dress away as if he were unwrapping a gift.

"All yours." My voice had gone high and breathless as he stripped me bare.

Aaron picked me up easily and held me like I weighed nothing. He stalked with me

across the room and tossed me onto the bed.

His bright blue eyes gazed down at me hungrily, never breaking eye contact, as he pulled off his shirt in one motion. All my attention was locked on the stretch of those muscles. The strength within his powerful body.

As he pulled his belt loose, freeing himself, I couldn't help but lick my lips at the sight of his thick cock. Aaron took himself in hand, stroking up and down his length as he stared slowly along my naked body. Tracing me with his eyes as he removed the last of his clothing.

My mouth parted. He was just so damn handsome. I couldn't think around him. He absolutely made me lose my mind.

Aaron climbed on to the bed and took my mouth in a rough kiss. My lips parted under his as our tongues battled for control. He tasted like sweet spices and desire. The weight of his body on top of me, brushing and sliding against me—he was perfect.

One large hard was cradled against my face. Touching me gently like I was precious. The other drifted lower between my thighs. His hand slid across my stomach to my wet core, where he pressed in a slow, circular pattern. His steady rhythm soon had me writhing.

Aaron swallowed my moans with his kisses.

Holding firm with that steady pattern, Aaron was absolutely unrelenting. My breath hitched. My clit was aching for more of his touch. I ground my hips against the press of his hand. Close, and desperate for the push that would take me over the edge.

Aaron began to kiss down my neck, trailing down to my breasts. His lips sealed around the taut peak of my nipple. He latched on. Sucking hard.

I gasped, breaking. Shattering. Losing myself in waves of white-hot pleasure that rippled from my core to every limb. My legs shook from the strength of it.

"Fuck." Aaron looked up at me sharply.

His expression was strained, with something wild and possessive. As if he was holding on to his control by the weakest thread.

He looked into my eyes, seeking permission. I held his gaze as I spread my legs wider for him.

Aaron's breath hitched, and his pupils darkened as he took in the sight of me. I was laid out before him. All his for the taking.

He lined up with me and slammed inside in one hard thrust.

My back arched, taking him deeper. I groaned at the stretch as muscles deep within me parted for him.

He settled his larger body over mine, kissing me sweetly on the lips before he began to move.

Aaron took me fast. Grasping on to my hips hard

enough to bruise, slamming into me so hard that I moved up the bed.

My moans got higher pitched. The feel of him moving so fast within me—it was incredible. It was like something wild was released inside of me. Something primal and untamed. I grasped at the shifting wall of muscles at his back, clutching hard enough to mark him. My nails bit into his skin as I held on.

It felt like holding on to a force of nature more than a man. His thrusts were fierce, absolutely brutal, and I wouldn't have it any other way.

He fucked me like he was trying to break through the barriers between us. Hard enough to make me feel the connection between us. To bind us together. He fucked me like he had something to prove.

In all that fast-moving friction, amidst all the pleasure between us, I felt the pleasure shift within me, almost crystalizing, as it built higher and higher.

His solid body slammed into me again and again. Pressing himself in deep, holding me close in his rugged grip. His fierce gaze never left me. Wild and possessive. Watching for the moment that my breath hitched and my jaw went slack. For the moment that I ground my hips against his in an urgent need for more.

"Aaron, please," I called out to him. Pleading for something that I couldn't quite put into words. Something just out of reach.

He didn't stop. Just kept up his hard pace. Relentless. Winding up the pressure that had been building within me. Until it was all consuming. Until it was everything. All of me boiled down to this one coiling mass of pleasure that kept rising.

I burst into white-hot pleasure.

Stars flared beneath my eyelids. Molten bliss erupted from my core, flooding every part of me. Moaning out his name, I closed my eyes. Contentment rippled through every pore of my body, and I was lost to it. As my every limb shuddered and relaxed.

Aaron's rhythm became harsher. Faster and almost jerky as he raced to his own completion.

He let out a low groan, grinding his hips into mine hard. I could feel him throbbing deep against my cervix. Rocking insistently against me with each pulse. He gripped me hard enough to leave bruises as his cock filled me completely.

When he finished, Aaron buried his head against my shoulder as his body slumped against mine and he went still. I stroked along his back, drawing invisible patterns and pictures across his skin. Tracing a child-like rendition of the house I grew up in. The curves of the bushes, longer strokes for the oak tree in the front yard.

I would typically stir at this point. Once the heaviness got to be too much, I would move just enough to get the full weight of his body off me. Instead, I stayed still, just enjoying the moment of connection between us.

I stopped stroking his back as I heard him snoring lightly against my ear. I smiled, smoothing down his hair, brushing along his head carefully.

It hit me then. This feeling—what it meant.

I was halfway in love with him.

I was well on the way to loving him.

At the realization, I stiffened. As I lay there, under the enemy I all but loved, still filled with his cock and with his semen.

24

AARON

I was halfway through a pile of reports, scanning for any sign of political movements, trying to figure out which groups would be interested in harming Sofia—which was harder to spot than I had anticipated since people's motivations seemed to all but disappear when they were written on official reports—when Mother burst into the room without knocking.

"Aaron." Her tone was harsh, and even through her thick vanilla and clove perfume, I could smell blood on her fingertips where wolf claws burst through.

I made a show of finishing the section that I was reading and placing the report down carefully on my desk. I leaned back in my chair carefully before regarding Mother.

I was playing the same game that she had played. She could be the first to start the conversation. Perhaps this time I could be the one to blindside her.

"You've been avoiding me." Mother glared at me just as she had done when I was young and she had caught me up to some mischief.

"I've been busy." I pointed to the piles of paperwork that I'd skimmed through.

"Too busy to meet your mother for tea?"

I didn't take the bait. Those meetings were never purely social visits, no matter that she wanted to pretend otherwise.

"What is this about?" I asked. Though I knew that whatever it was, it couldn't be good. Mother had never resorted to barging into my office when I was in the middle of work before. Our last conversation left behind a sense of tension that was hanging over every word between us.

"Aaron, I didn't want it to have to come to this. But you aren't thinking straight. The way that you have been acting hasn't been normal. You refuse to see reason." The look that she gave me was half pained. As if it were hurting *her* to say it. But the expression on her face didn't match. The strain of storming through the castle made her sweat off some of her perfume.

Within me, my wolf was on high alert. There was something off about Mother. The scents breaking through her cloaking perfumes were alarming—there was an acidic tinge to her sweat. Sour, and chemically unbalanced.

It wasn't a sickness. Whatever was in Mother's system wasn't natural. *Drugs.* She shouldn't have to take them medicinally. Not as a shifter. Was she taking them for fun? How long had this been going on?

She met my gaze. "I'm not going to watch you lose your status. Not over some River wolf."

"What have you done?" I asked slowly, a gritty edge to every word.

"I have made arrangements with the Hansen family. They are willing to work to smooth out your indiscretions."

What the fuck?

Indiscretions? Was she talking about my relationship with Sofia? Like my soulbond was nothing more than some torrid affair?

What did she mean by arrangements? I knew that she was suggesting that I give up Sofia for the Hansen girl. But what did she mean by smooth out indiscretions? That sounded like she was planning on harming Sofia directly. But Mother couldn't threaten her. Not when that would potentially start a war.

"Why do you think that I'll agree to any of this? I told you before that I don't want anyone else." I said each word slowly. Without knowing exactly what Mother had up her sleeve, I had to tread with caution... Maybe if I admitted a bit of what Sofia meant to me, I could soften Mother's opinion. Make her back down. "I honestly thought that you would be happy for me. I'm happy with her. I want to be with her."

"My son." Mother brought her fingertips to my cheek, stroking lightly against my jaw. "I know that you don't want to see it. But this match would be political suicide. Whoever you claim by your side will be in the second highest position of power in the entire pack. None of the Stonevalley wolves will accept a River wolf as their alpha's mate." Her fingers dug into my face along with her accusations. "You need to think of the long-term consequences. You have to understand that you are throwing your people into chaos. This could divide the pack. They could revolt against you, possibly even kill you to overthrow your rule."

My hands were clenched at my sides as I held myself very still. My wolf was snarling within my mind. He was aware of a threat to his mate. The fact that he was unsure of where the threat was coming from was only making him more vicious.

What Mother was saying might be true. But I refused to believe that leaving Sofia was the only solution. The thought of putting my hands on a woman other than Sofia turned my stomach so sharply it made me want to gag.

Leaving my mate? The other half of my soul? The one chosen for me by the goddess herself? There was no fucking way that could possibly be right.

Mother sighed, as if she could hear exactly what I was thinking.

When she looked at me, a hint of sorrow pooled in the corners of her eyes. "I wish that things were different. If the alpha was in a stronger condition. If you weren't born to take his place. If you were just anyone, yes, I could agree that you should follow your heart. But you aren't anyone. You are the heir to the alpha. Your pack needs you."

The finality in her tone grated at me.

"You forget that I haven't given you an answer. I haven't agreed to anything."

She gave me a pitying look. "You don't have a choice. I've already spoken to the alpha. It's a done deal."

I stood rooted to the spot. Mother had convinced the alpha to keep me from my mate? To marry me to some other girl? In the pack, the law of the alpha was absolute.

The only way to escape one of his direct commands would be through leaving the pack. Leaving them without a proper leader. Leaving them vulnerable and defenseless. I couldn't even take her with me. Sofia had to stay at Stonevalley castle, as per the terms of the treaty.

Basically, I was fucked.

"I understand that this isn't what you want to hear. But as long as you are properly married to an acceptable bride, it may be possible for you to keep your little mate as a mistress. We can make arrangements."

Mother patted my arm, just the same as she had done when I was a child and she told me that my pet goose had died. Not at all like a woman informing her grown son that she had taken away his freedom and choice in the most important decision in his life.

Did Mother actually think that I would be okay with all of this so long as I got to tarnish Sofia's dignity and have her as my kept woman? If so, she had no idea the power Sofia had, hidden just below the surface.

It was ironic. If I had been soulmated to any other girl in this castle, Mother would never have questioned it. Mother would have never treated any other girl with such disrespect. Though she was quiet about it, my mate had one of the fiercest hearts out of anyone who lived here. Mother misjudged Sofia entirely; my mate was more than the circumstances of her blood.

I pulled my arm away from where Mother continued to stroke at my skin, disgusted.

"I can promise you this. If you do manage to force me into marrying some other woman, I'll never touch her. And I will never speak to you again."

I clutched the porcelain rim of the toilet seat, certain that I must have emptied out the entire content of my stomach, when I puked once more. My stomach heaved as vomit erupted out of me. When it was over, I spat into the toilet bowl and struggled to catch my breath. I could barely stir to get away from the bitter stench of my own sick.

What the hell was wrong with me?

I'd woken up with a headache intense enough that I decided to skip my classes for the day. But only forty minutes later, I found myself hurling into the toilet bowl.

I hadn't eaten anything unusual. Peach oatmeal and black tea for breakfast. Last night, I had a tray brought up for dinner. The meal was mostly chicken and potatoes, all cooked properly. Nothing that would make me vomit. I didn't even have any wine.

The thought crawled up the back of my head, itching to the front of my mind. Nefarious and persistent. I knew one thing that could cause me to be throwing up right now.

No.

It wasn't possible. Why did I do these things to myself?

It was like I was willingly letting my own mind harass me. It wasn't possible.

Wait. Was it?

When was the last time I had had my period?

I held my hand to my temple as I realized that the last time I could recall having my monthly courses was sometime before I shifted for the first time.

A pit dropped into the center of my hollowed-out stomach.

That didn't necessarily mean anything. I got the talk, just the same as the other potential wolves as part of our biologics curriculum. It was a common fact that shifter menstruation was irregular. I didn't have to jump to any conclusions.

As a shifter, the chances that I would get pregnant were about the same as a human on the pill. Not that birth control would work on me. The change from woman into wolf broke down and reconstructed my entire body. It would burn the hormones right out of my system. Besides, changing into the wolf and back into a human acted like a hard reset on ovulation. If I shifted enough, I wouldn't ovulate at all.

It took some wolves decades to conceive.

Though it wasn't as if there were no chance of pregnancy, the numbers were just so slim that I didn't think of it.

Besides, Aaron and I were both shifters.

Wolves were no longer getting pregnant.

There hadn't been a child conceived between shifters in over twenty years in the Stonevalley castle. Aaron himself had been the last one born. It was the unspoken problem that had plagued both of the packs. None of the River wolf shifters had been able to conceive in over a decade and a half as well. There was always a possibility that the wolf shifter gene could come from the other humans in the pack. The odds were somewhat smaller, but it still happened. They still had it in their bloodline.

Even if the wolf shifters were somehow able to bear children again, it didn't make sense that it would start with me. Why would I be the one to beat the slim odds? Even if I could, it hadn't been enough time. Yes, Aaron and I had been having quite a lot of sex. But things worked differently for shifters. It hadn't been enough time for something like a pregnancy.

I pulled myself to my feet and caught a glimpse of my stomach in my bathroom mirror. I lifted up my chemise blouse and took a hard look at the flat planes of my belly—it certainly didn't look any different. There was no visible bump or anything like that. It looked too small for anything to ever fit in there.

A soft knock at the door jarred me out of my thoughts. When Aaron had left in the morning, he'd mentioned that he needed to get some work done today. Maybe he had ended up cutting it short to come check on me. He must have realized by now that I hadn't gone to class.

I opened my door to reveal the exact same hue of Aaron's brilliant eyes in a different face. Staring down at me coldly. It was Lady Ragnolf, the alpha's mate, flanked by two generals. Her fine blonde hair was elaborately braided, and she was dressed in royal attire—long embroidered silk with fur trimmings, in a royal purple that showed off her powerful figure. She didn't look a day over twenty-five, though she was in fact much older. As the alpha no longer made regular appearances in public, she was effectively the most powerful shifter authority in the castle.

She was also currently staring at me as if she had been

searching for the source of an unpleasant smell, and it had been coming from me all along.

What did she want from me? Was this about my academic attendance?

No, the matriarch of an entire pack wouldn't concern herself with a few missed classes. At least, she had never ventured to my rooms before in the past five years.

What could make her start now?

I hastily stepped away from the door to allow her to enter.

As her gaze locked onto my bare forearm, I realized my mistake. My soulmark was uncovered and exposed. All of the dark swirls and geometric patterns of it stood on display. Just like that, one moment of carelessness and my secret was out.

But by the way she was narrowing her eyes at my soulmark, it was as if she already knew—knew, but didn't like what she was seeing.

I fumbled into a clumsy curtsy as she stepped into my room. "Lady Ragnolf."

Lady Ragnolf sniffed the air in my room once sharply then held her chin high, as if holding her nose up and away from the stench. I knew exactly what she was sensing. My room smelled strongly of Aaron and sex. Now the odor had lingering notes of vomit wafting in through my closed bathroom door.

I stood stock-still directly in the center of my room, making no explanations or apologies. It was painfully obvious that Aaron and I were together. There was no hiding it. If the good Lady Ragnolf did not want to walk into the scent of her son's copulation, then perhaps she shouldn't have barged into my room unannounced.

"It has come to my attention that you have seduced my

son. After we have brought you here and treated you as one of our own. Provided for your education and clothing, everything that you could possibly need." Lady Ragnolf narrowed her eyes at me, as if she would much prefer not having to look at me at all.

What was she accusing me of doing? Seducing him? All right, so I might have done a little seducing, but it wasn't like that. I didn't understand why she was so angry about my actions when the truth of the matter was written directly into my skin. The truth was exposed for anyone with eyes to see it.

"He's my soulmate."

"You may have confused him with these old traditions, but mark my words. You are not worthy of my son. You have never been fit to be with him in any official capacity."

I swallowed. The evidence to the contrary was wafting around in the air all around us. I stated the obvious. "We've already been together."

"Obviously." Lady Ragnolf rolled her eyes. "My son finds you fit for fucking, if for nothing else."

If she had walked across the room and slapped me across the face, it would have shocked me less.

"I don't know what sweet words he might have told you, but I'm here to set matters straight." She stepped closer to me with the slow gait of a predator, flanked on each side by generals with killing experience. I recognized General Albertsen, who loomed closer with a grim expression. I was outnumbered, and once again too slow to realize the danger I was in. "Do you think that my son wants to be publicly associated with someone like you?"

I swallowed. I wanted to set her straight. That it had been my decision to hide our relationship and that Aaron had been respecting my wishes. But the truth sounded watery and small when confronted with the hatred blazing in the depths of Lady Ragnolf's eyes.

My wolf rose to the surface. To my wolf, this woman was making loud noise that didn't mean anything. If her mate had a problem, she would believe it from his lips. Not from anyone else's.

"Yes," I said, treating it like an honest question rather than as the threat that she had intended it to be.

Her eyes flashed with malice and a hint of something else. "Then why has he already agreed to a marriage proposal to someone else?"

My mouth snapped shut. What could I say to that? I wanted to tell her that she didn't know what she was talking about. That Aaron would never agree to marrying someone who wasn't his mate. But all I knew was what he had told me. Why should I presume to know what Aaron wanted more than his own mother?

Maybe words whispered in the dark didn't hold as much weight in the light of day.

Lady Ragnolf circled closer, eyeing me for weaknesses as if I were injured prey. "You may have had a comfortable life here so far, but just remember, all of that could change. If you want to hold on to the right to see my son, if you wish to allow him to continue to enjoy your body, we may be able to come to a certain understanding. As long as you remember exactly what you are. As long as you never forget your place."

26

AARON

I ran through some excuses to tell Sofia's instructors to get her away from her classes. None of them sounded right. Fuck it. I'd just waltz in and tell her that she was needed and take her away. I had to warn Sofia that Mother was planning something. So that she wouldn't be blindsided if Mother tried to get her claws in her.

From outside of the classroom, I could tell that something was off. All I could smell through the doors was human. The scent of my mate had taken on a brightness that I could pick out anywhere. The human part of her was light and feminine. The almost fruity and sensual notes of jasmine. The scent of the wolf lying just under the surface was something earthy and wild.

She wasn't in class today. Her presence was completely absent, besides the traces of her from the last time she had visited this room. That scent seemed days old. She also didn't seem to be anywhere in the surrounding area.

I kept walking down the corridor, passing Sofia's classroom. If she wasn't sticking to her normal routine, she could be anywhere in the castle.

Mother was acting like my choice to be with Sofia would do more than bring about my downfall. She'd told me that my decision would throw the pack into chaos.

None of this was fucking fair.

Growing up, my life was my own. There was none of this pressure. None of this scrutiny. I never had to consider the weight of leadership. Not until the treaty was signed and Erik was taken away.

My brother was made to be a leader. He was the eldest. The responsible one. He had always lived and breathed the rules. When he was next in line to become the alpha, I was free to train as I wished. I could focus on whatever interests suited me.

Every year since my brother was traded away, the weight of my title only grew heavier. This year more than ever, my life had been buried in paperwork. In navigating political intricacies. I knew that the Stonevalley wolves needed a leader. The pack needed my protection and strength. I'd already sacrificed for them, and I would continue to do it. I could take up that mantle and be what they needed me to be. It was the path that was written in my blood.

Duty to my people was never meant to come at the price of my own happiness. It was never supposed to cost me my soulmate. To open up my chest and see if I would rip out my heart in exchange for my responsibilities.

No one else had my history and bloodline. My position as the alpha's heir was uncontested. But I couldn't just appoint my cousin who was my closest relation. If I stepped down from my role, it would open the floodgates. It would allow anyone power-thirsty enough to take the opportunity to fight to rule. It would come at the cost of the blood of wolves we could not afford.

Our pack absolutely could not lose any more wolves. If our numbers got any lower, our vulnerability would become obvious. It would be an open invitation to other wolf packs who wanted to expand their territories and take control.

I didn't even want the role. Didn't care about the prestige of it. All I wanted was to live with my soulmate in peace. In order to fulfill my duty, I couldn't even have that? How was I supposed to live with myself if I turned my back on the woman I wanted to be with?

How could it be possible for my duty to require me to lose the other half of my soul?

Losing her wasn't an option. Being forced to marry another woman? Just to avoid the political fallout of our match? It wasn't happening. I didn't know who the fuck Mother thought that she was, trying to control who I married. Did she think that she could make a choice for me better than the gods themselves?

Enough was enough. It was time for me to deal with this head on. It was time to confront the alpha.

27

SOFIA

As soon as my door softly closed and Lady Ragnolf slipped quietly out of my room, my brain switched gears from barely processing anything to having everything from the last few hours come crashing down.

My thoughts started to swim. Like I was drowning. All the furniture, decorations, everything in my room started to blur together.

If Lady Ragnolf was this angry that I was having a relationship with her son, what would she do to me once she found out that I could be pregnant?

What if I was actually pregnant?

My hands trembled at my sides, and I couldn't get them to stop. I couldn't push the thought out of my mind. Of my body contorting and swelling. Filled with a baby, vulnerable as wet paper.

I could just picture it. Another little girl, small like me. Trying to press herself as tight as she could against the walls of the castle so that no one could spot her. So that nobody would look at her too closely and snarl at her. Like she was nothing better than a piece of meat.

How could I protect a child when I was powerless to even protect myself?

The words of Lady Ragnolf lingered. Whispering hatefully from the hidden shadows in my mind. Refusing to go away.

He finds you fit for fucking, if for nothing else. He already agreed to a marriage proposal to someone else.

What if Lady Ragnolf was right?

What if Aaron wanted to use my body and nothing more? And I was the only one too blind to see the truth of it?

Until the moment we'd soulbonded, Aaron was convinced that I was spying on his family. Just a few months ago I'd crossed paths with him in the upper hallways on the way to my alpha politics class. Aaron had been carrying a stack of paperwork. As soon as he saw me, Aaron tensed. He straightened like I was a threat.

"Turn. Around."

His words had been low and laced with a command I had no choice but to follow. Forcing me to turn and walk away from him, and take the long way around the castle. Even though changing course had made me late to my class. Even though I'd never been a spy and the whole thing was ridiculous.

It was like dealing with a completely different person. But it wasn't a different person.

Was it really that impossible to believe that someone who had always seen me as untrustworthy wouldn't want to be in an official relationship with me?

If he had already agreed to marry someone more suitable, how would he take the news that I could be pregnant? What if he didn't even want this child? A little lost baby, with nothing but one scrawny mother who could barely keep herself alive.

How could I protect a child when I was utterly, utterly alone here?

I was numb. Cold as ice. My feet moved without me paying attention to them. Walking up to the door of my room and stepping out. Down the stone corridor, with one hand trailing across the rough walls. Completely on autopilot.

How could I have been so stupid? I was mixing my bloodline with that of the Stonevalley pack. As if that could result in anything other than someone who would never fit in anywhere—a baby who would never grow to have a true place to call their home.

How could I do this to my own child?

Without a plan, without paying any attention to where I was going, I found myself at the base of the castle, near the stables and the back doorway. I paused, shaking against the latch on the door, before quietly opening it and stepping outside.

The wind rushed against my face, pulling my long hair out of its delicate braid. Goosebumps dotted all the way up my arms. Ignoring the walkways and streaking my velvet flats with mud, I walked far from the Stonevalley castle until I was surrounded by the old growth trees in the forest.

I felt like I was going into shock. Like an unseen part of myself was cut open and something vital within me was draining out. Leaking away. Gone.

My wolf watched me anxiously. She could feel all the pain lancing into me. Wounds threatening to destroy me. Aware of my panic. Of the all-consuming fear that pounded through my veins, numbing me into indecision. She was panting and pacing. Ready to charge at this unknown enemy, even though she couldn't quite understand it.

She had seen enough.

I fell to the ground as my body split open in pain. As the wolf took over.

I ran, and the trees and foliage streaked into blurs of movement around me as my paws tore into the land. I had to move faster than I could think. Faster than my heart. Before I came to terms with the fact that every racing step took me farther and farther away from warm arms and bright blue eyes that were the closest thing to a home that I had ever known.

I didn't think, I just ran. Because I had to. Because there was no other choice.

I didn't stop until I reached land that smelled like pine and safety. Until I could sense the faint smell of my mother, my own father. Traces of my sister in the wind.

I closed my eyes, savoring the feel of the land I grew up in. Home was so close I could practically taste it. The bitter grounds of father's dark roast coffee. Ash and melted lavender wax. Sage. Lemon cleaner. All the cooking spices. Turmeric. Cayenne pepper. Oregano and basil.

I hadn't seen any of them or spoken to any of them in so many years. The last time I was just a kid. All of a sudden, the only thing I wanted was to be in my mother's arms, to have her hold me. To tell me that everything was going to be all right. That I was safe. That no one was going to hurt me.

I leapt into the river dividing the two territories and I didn't hesitate. I hit the water, ignoring the shock of cold.

Cold that tore through my fur, piercing into my skin. Cold waves that dragged at me.

I didn't stop until I reached the shore. For the first time in years, my paws touched my native soil. This was it. I had broken the treaty. Without stopping to think of the consequences.

"I was about to kill you outright, before I realized who you are," a deep yet oddly familiar voice called out to me.

A voice that stopped me in my tracks.

My wolf cocked her ears at the sound. His voice was so much more than just a voice.

I was stopped by the sight of a face that I had longed to see. One that I thought I had left behind. Bright blue eyes. A strong square jaw. It was Aaron, only it wasn't. Knowing the face so intimately, I could immediately spot differences. The shape of his head was slightly broader, and he had grown his hair out longer. Braiding it in the style of my people.

This wasn't Aaron. This was the boy who I had traded places with those five years ago. This was Erik. Aaron's brother. Though he was clearly not a boy any longer. He was broad chested now and thickly muscled like his brother. All grown up and aiming a weapon at me.

He had nocked an arrow, pointing the metal edge of it to the ground. From the gray glint of the metal, I could tell that it was tipped with silver. If he'd used it on me, I would have been dead before even realizing what was happening.

The coloring of my wolf must have given Erik pause. Black fur was more common among River wolves. It wasn't a shade found on any of living Stonevalley wolf. Except for one now.

I wasn't thinking.

All of a sudden, this felt like nothing more than another mistake in the series of bad decisions that I had made.

My wolf was powerless to defend herself. To explain what she was doing here. I needed to change back to my human form.

Colors shifted, blazing sharper. Brighter. The scents in the forest muted until the smells of my family, the friends I had grown up with, all faded away. Then came the pain. The sharp crack of bones twisting. Reforming. Muscles that twisted into place until the wolf was within me once more.

Finally, the chill of the wind on my bare skin as I reformed on my native soil. Completely naked.

I crossed my arms over my chest, covering myself as best as I could before meeting Erik's wary blue eyes. Though the shape and color were so familiar to me, I found no sympathy within them. "Please, I just want to go home."

"Then you are going the wrong way. You will need to turn around and head back in the direction you came from." Erik nodded back toward the Stonevalley castle.

"I don't mean any harm. I didn't come here to hurt anyone. I haven't seen my family in so long. Please. I just want to see them." It had been years since I had come within a mile of my family. Hadn't even been able to speak to them. Was Grandmother all right? I heard whispers that new wolves turned. Was it anyone that I knew? My sister wasn't quite of age, but wolf shifting sometimes came slightly early. Was it her? Had she shifted?

"But they aren't your family. Not anymore." Erik shook his head slowly, as if he was talking to someone who was slow to understand a basic truth. His words were sharp and piercing as his weapon, and they hit their mark with just the same brutal efficiency. "Whether you like it or not, you are bound by the rules of the treaty. You cannot be here."

It felt as if the hope within me had deflated.

To have come so close, only to be turned away.

By the very man who'd replaced me. A man who looked more at ease in my former role than I ever had before the trade.

Maybe I was always meant to be an outsider.

I hunched in on myself as a gust of wind blew against my still damp skin. I wanted to be wrapped in one of grandmother's woven blankets as she grabbed me a hot chocolate and told me stories about the old wolves. I wrapped my arms tightly around myself as if I could hold in all of the emotions threatening to spill out. I wasn't safe here. This wasn't the place where I could break down and cry.

Erik sighed, lowering his weapon to the ground. "What about your soulmate?" He gestured to the mark exposed on my bare arms.

I clutched my mark, covering it with my palm, though the damage was already done. So much for holding on to my secrets.

I might not have been able to turn to the River wolves any longer, but I still had my soulmate. Could I still count on Aaron? I squeezed my eyes shut, unsure. I wanted to press my hand over my belly protectively. I had already screwed things up in so many ways. I couldn't afford to be careless now. Not when it could be putting a new life in danger.

I probably shouldn't have said anything. Erik was right. I shouldn't be here. There was too much at stake, the consequences were too great, and I'd made enough of a mess already. But I just didn't know what else to do.

"I'm in trouble." I barely whispered the words. As if I was afraid to say them out loud. As if releasing them into the air could make them truer. "I think I might be pregnant."

Erik froze, his gaze dropping to my flat stomach. He tilted his head in a wolf-like gesture as he considered me.

Was he close enough to tell that his brother was my mate? That I was carrying the Stonevalley alpha's bloodline? Third in line to take power? I was downwind, and far enough away that he might not be able to catch the scent.

Even without knowing who my mate was, Erik had to have found it strange for a pregnant wolf to be on the run. That was almost unheard of. Soulmates typically became more protective during pregnancy.

Erik had no reason to help me. There wasn't any home left for me to run back to.

After a long moment, he nodded to himself. Decision made.

"About a half mile west, near the large rock formation, there's a drop box. It's got some clothes that should be in your size, and an emergency cash box. I'm the main patrol out tonight. So long as you are quick about it, no one'll bother you."

I nodded eagerly, opening my mouth to thank him.

Erik cut me off before I got the chance. Watching me with every word to make sure that his message got across.

"Just remember that this land is no longer your home. If you come back, I'll have to shoot you."

28

AARON

I tensed at the door, unsure of what version of the alpha I would face today. When he opened it, I was greeted with a nod of acknowledgement.

The alpha pulled out a chair and sat at his desk across from me.

Was this muscle memory? Or did he actually recognize me? Was this a good day? There were days when the alpha had forgotten that he had ever sired children. Other days, he would forget about the treaty entirely and ask for Erik.

The alpha was old. Centuries older than any other wolf in the pack. He'd been old when he finally found his soulmate and bonded to Mother. Old when he'd sired me and raised me. Growing up, he was like a pillar of strength. He was consistent. Indestructible.

While his body may be the strongest of any of the wolves in the pack, his mind was still human.

The human mind was not designed to survive for hundreds of years.

The decline was gradual, but it started to accelerate a little less than a year ago. The pack doctors compared the deterioration to Alzheimer's. They said that it was degenerative, and that there was nothing that they could do.

In humans, diseases of the mind typically impacted the elderly. It was a completely different matter when dealing with the battered mind of a man who could transform into a one-hundred-and-fifty-pound wolf.

Recently, the breaks from reality had gotten more dangerous. He'd managed to slip past the guards posted by his room—guards who couldn't do much more than report back. No one at the castle was really equipped to stop the most physically powerful and dominant wolf.

When he'd gotten out last month, he'd flirted with a woman at least three hundred years younger than him. Mother had had to intervene. Pretending to meet him for the first time, as he didn't even remember that he'd ever had a mate. Other times he'd run off and sparred with some of the younger generals. The alpha had nearly killed them. If they hadn't been wolves, they'd have been dead.

It was hard to see him like this. Strong as ever, but forgetting himself. Trapped by his own mind.

Perhaps it was because the disease was invisible. Because it wasn't possible for me to see the damage that had fractured his mind. Because he looked like a man in perfect health. It was getting harder and harder for me to tamper down my feelings of disgust.

My emotions were just stronger than my ability to be rational.

I fought to keep a neutral expression on my face. Pressed my palm hard against my knee, though I wanted to release my claws and dig them into my own flesh and let the pain keep me grounded. I breathed deeply instead. If the alpha smelled blood on me, it could set him off.

He lined up each of the pens on his desk until all of

them were perfectly vertical in front of him. Was that normal? I never scrutinized his organizational habits. They'd never mattered before. I never would have imagined that the way the alpha managed his writing utensils could be the key to figuring out how to save my relationship with my soulmate.

I should have been spending more time with the alpha than ever. Learning as much as I could from all the years of wisdom he could still pass down. Instead, I avoided the man as much as possible—a man who still looked to be in his prime, but who could have a breakdown and make messes like a child.

This delicate balance between the alpha and the alpha's heir was not sustainable. Traditionally, alphas remained in power for as long as they were physically strong enough to hold the position. The alpha of the Stonevalley wolves— despite his illness—was still in peak physical condition.

Things could only become more strained between us.

"Aaron, it's been too long."

I breathed a sigh of relief before nodding to him respectfully. It was a good day, then. He was lucid enough today to remember me.

I wouldn't have been able to trust it if he'd called me 'my son.' I'd spoken to him before thinking that everything was fine, only for him to address me later as Erik. Now I knew for certain he knew who I was. A kernel of hope flickered to life within me.

He pointed over to a stack of paperwork I sent over to him. "I looked over your reports. It seems like you have a strong handle on affairs."

I nodded, swallowing. I had to take on the majority of the paperwork for the alpha.

"I actually came to discuss a more personal matter." I

kept my tone even. Though the topic of conversation felt like a lit match within me, threatening to burn me down from the inside.

The best thing to do would have been to approach the situation with caution, ease the alpha into the topic. But I couldn't help the rage that simmered below the surface. "Did Mother tell you that I found my soulmate?"

"Congratulations." The alpha leaned in, clasping my shoulder. "The goddess must be pleased with you. It was years before she blessed me with the mark of my soulmate."

His voice was jolly and bright. He didn't sound like he'd heard the news at all. Then again, with the alpha, I'd had to learn not to put any stock into his short-term memory.

"Did Mother tell you who my soulmate is?"

"I'm not sure." The alpha shrugged his shoulder, but within his expression, a hint of worry flickered.

I wonder if he even knew that his memory had turned into a stack of cards.

"It's Sofia," I admitted. I said her name as objectively as I could in order to gauge his reaction.

"Aaron." The alpha pressed his lips into a thin line.

Every muscle in my body tensed. This was the alpha. If he gave me a direct order concerning my mate, I would have to obey him. Or fight him.

The alpha sighed heavily. "You aren't thinking of rejecting her, are you?"

All the thoughts in my head ground down to a halt.

"What?" This was not a turn of events I had been expecting at *all*.

"Your mother and I taught you better than that. The girl might seem scrappy and small. But there is strength in her blood. She might have been born on the wrong side of the river, but you have to remember that this girl is an alpha's daughter." The alpha narrowed his eyes at me as he lectured me. Repeating back to me the whole chain of thoughts that I'd had to process when I first made the decision to have her. "Besides, there is a reason why the moon goddess chooses as she chooses. There must be something more to the girl than meets the eye."

I had come prepared to fight for *her*. Just to find the alpha coming to her defense instead.

"I know. I'm in love with her."

As soon as the words slipped out of my mouth, I realized that they were true. I was in love with Sofia. I had been, for longer than I had realized.

I didn't know exactly when the feeling had started. But now that I could identify this emotion raging in my chest at the thought of her taken away from me, I could recognize it. I was in love with her. Had been for quite some time.

"Well, that's good, then." The alpha sat back down in his chair, folding his hands neatly in front of himself.

I tapped my finger against the table, trying to think through the best way to broach this subject. "Mother doesn't approve."

The alpha narrowed his eyes. "What's there to approve? Your match is your match. Does she have a problem with Sofia being your sister? You two aren't biologically related. You weren't raised together. That shouldn't matter."

"She barged into my office and demanded that I reject my mate. She wants me to marry the Hansen girl instead."

The alpha stared at me blankly, as if he were waiting for me to deliver a punchline. As if this was all nothing more than a bad joke. "Why the fuck would Astrid do that?"

"Mother told me that the pack would never accept the match. That I would destroy my credibility and cause the people to rebel against me."

The alpha shook his head slowly. "Your mother forgets herself. Has lost sight of the bigger picture in the middle of all the politics. There is political upheaval because of the lack of wolves. If we can increase the number of wolves, the humans will fall in line. They always do. Rejecting the will of the goddess is the absolute worst decision for the alpha of a pack."

I held my temple. If this was how the alpha really felt, how could have things gotten so twisted? "She told me that she ran it by you. That you sanctioned her idea of marrying me off."

The alpha looked away, staring hard at nothing in particular as he considered my words. He shook his head. "Aaron, I don't think that my memory's working like it used to."

I swallowed as I clenched my teeth together. It was almost harder to hear him like this. Rational, and only vaguely aware that something was wrong. It was too strong of a reminder of how things used to be.

"What do you suggest? What should I say to Mother?"

The alpha drummed his fingers against the tabletop. A smirk flit across his face, making him look younger. "Bring your soulmate here. If your mother wants you to have a wedding, then let's have a wedding."

I burst into Sofia's room, using my spare key rather than knocking.

"Sofia?"

Adrenaline coursed through every inch of my veins. I'd been granted a reprieve from the worst possible news. This news, however, came attached to a verifiable time bomb. How long would the alpha remain lucid? What would I do if he forgot his offer to marry us?

A wedding officiated by the alpha would be a quick affair, but still legally binding.

This might not even be what she wanted. Sofia was still hung up on her privacy. That was fine if that was what she needed. We could keep our relationship private. I could agree to having a secret marriage with her. Whatever she wanted. As long as I could keep her.

This wasn't the romantic proposal that my girl deserved. She deserved a full celebration. A ceremony in her honor. A huge rock on her finger. She deserved to be recognized in front of everyone as my mate. Instead, I planned to barge into her room and whisk her away in a rush.

But compared to the alternative? Compared to the possibility of losing her? Of having to run with her, potentially starting a war? Letting the pack dissolve into anarchy? I had to take advantage of this offer while I still could. Before Mother could push through her own plans to coerce me into accepting a politically advantageous union.

Sofia wasn't in her bed. Crossing the room, I checked her bathroom only to find that it was empty as well.

I had to face the facts. Sofia wasn't here.

I was too late.

The room was completely empty, except for the scent of vanilla and clove that hung in the air, covering everything.

No.

What had Mother done?

29

SOFIA

I found the storage container exactly where Erik said it would be. That didn't surprise me. Erik looked like the sort of man to keep his word. I unlatched the security box to stacks of clothing.

As soon as I opened the lid, I recognized her scent. Like rain and rosewater. Like grass stains and dirt under finger-nails. Even the faint aroma of butterscotch hard candies that were her absolute favorites. The drop off container smelled exactly like I remembered my sister.

My fingers darted to the middle pile, to a faded purple T-shirt that I could distantly remember her wear-ing. I pulled the fabric up to my nose, smelling deeply. There was no mistake about it. The shirt was hers, with another layer of smells just below the surface. A scent that was wild. A scent of fur and fangs, with hints of the forest.

My little sister was growing up without me.

The corners of my eyes filled with moisture. I wished that I could talk to her about it. Run through the forest with her. Ask her what she thought about being a wolf. When she was little, we would tease each other about soulmates. Wonder together what they would be like.

I looked up into the sky, holding back tears. She was a shifter, like I always knew she would be. I just wished that I could have been there. Seen her through her first transformation. That I could be there for her and watch her enter into this whole new world.

I might never speak to her again.

This land would never again be my home.

I pulled the purple shirt over my head. It had a silly cartoon character of a dumpling winking. I breathed in the collar, taking her scent deeply. At least for now, I would have her close to me. While her scent remained.

I grabbed some faded jeans and worn-down sneakers before rummaging through the container for the stash of emergency money. There was a manila envelope wedged into the corner of the bin. Inside were stacks of bills. I hadn't had to use money in years and had no idea how much things cost in stores anymore. I took a small handful. Not sure if it would be enough, but scared to take too much.

Dressed once more, I closed the lid and relatched it firmly.

I leaned over the top of the plastic bin.

Where do I go now?

I couldn't stay here. Erik mentioned that the patrols would eventually change. I would only be able to pass through here unharrassed if I moved through quickly. I had to leave the territory. So where to go?

I hadn't exactly made a solid plan about leaving the castle. Hadn't thought things through. Though I was never treated like a prisoner, I'd known that I wasn't allowed to go far from the castle. I knew little about the layout of the land in the Stonevalley territory.

The land I grew up in was another story. A few miles west from here, there was a town right outside of the Edgeriver territory. I'd be able to pick up supplies there. It was as good a destination as any.

I placed my hand on my flat stomach and shivered.

I'd panicked after Lady Ragnolf cornered me with news about her son's upcoming nuptials. I thought that I was secure in my relationship with him, but all it took was a few solid threats for me to question everything.

What was worse, I lost control. I allowed the wolf to take over.

Fetuses were rarely able to survive the strain of a shifting mother. Transforming into a wolf could cause abortion.

I held my taut stomach, though there wasn't even a bump or anything to hold on to. I didn't mean to do it. Obviously I hadn't planned for a child to happen, but that didn't mean that I wanted the little one to come to any harm.

What if I'd lost both of them? Aaron and my child? All because of my own moment of weakness? If what Lady Ragnolf was saying about Aaron was true, he would be getting married to another woman. That would mean that this child in my belly could be the only link that I'd have to him. The only lingering connection to my soulmate. In one moment of panic, I could have thrown an entire life away.

I could always take a pregnancy test. If I had lost the child and shifted, the transformation to wolf should burn all the evidence of the changes in my body out of my system. But if my little one was still alive, the pregnancy hormones would remain.

Without shifting, though, it would be a long trek through the Edgeriver territory to get into town. I'd have to get a move on to make sure to avoid the patrol. I looked up at the afternoon sun and the wide stretch of forest left between me and the village. It was a long way to go on human feet. Though the wolf could cover the distance in minutes, I didn't dare transform a second time. I'd never risk my little one.

I had only been walking for half a mile when my stomach started to protest. Growing up, I was never so soft. I hadn't realized how my time at the Stonevalley castle had conditioned me to expect three square meals at regular hours.

Or could this be a sign of something else? Was this hunger I was feeling a sign of a small body developing within me? One that I had barely managed to keep alive and was now starving? I patted my stomach, giving it a silent promise that as soon as I was able, I'd get some food. I couldn't bring myself to think about what I would do if I was already too late.

The light of the sun was already starting to fade into the evening by the time I broke free of the forest that marked the edge of River territory. I stepped into a neighborhood of pristine suburban houses with neat white picket fences.

It had been years since I last visited this town. The convenience store might not even still be in business. I headed down the block toward it anyway, feet dragging. I'd had to walk through a rocky patch of the Edgeriver territory completely barefoot in order to get to their drop off box.

The store that my sister and I used to go to when we were kids was still open and looking exactly how I remembered. It used to feel like a little adventure, leaving the pack land and traveling here. Buying our snacks. It felt like I was walking straight out of one of my memories, or out of a dream of her, when I saw the exact same advertisements posted in the front of the store. The same fluorescent lights flickering from the ceiling. The same rows of snacks, with all the same brands of chips that I used to buy. I almost expected to look behind me to see my little sister trailing after me.

As soon as I entered the store, I headed straight for the snack aisle, grabbing the spicy Cheez-Its I hadn't eaten in years. Reaching for the jalapeño-flavored beef jerky strips and stopped. Would these snacks make me throw up again? Were they safe for an unborn child?

How much did all of this even cost?

I returned my favorites, though the ache in the hollow of my stomach was making me nauseous. I had priorities. First things first. I wandered through the aisles until I found health supplies. I wandered past cough drops and pain relief, scanning across the aisles until I found the pregnancy tests. Picking up the little pink box with shaky fingers, I turned it over in my hands until I was able to find the price tag.

I swallowed with numb relief when I saw that prices hadn't gone up crazy high since I was a kid. I didn't know what I was supposed to do if I didn't have enough money for the test. I didn't like the idea of stealing or going off and asking some stranger for help.

I brought the box and nothing else to the front of the store, ignoring the smirk on the young cashier's face as he rung me up. I didn't say anything as I peeled off bills that got slightly crumpled in my pocket to pay. Ignoring him, I grabbed my plastic bag and headed to the back of the store to the restroom.

Reading through all of the directions three times, I forced down large calming breaths. It was okay, I could do this. No matter what the outcome was, the important thing was knowing. I needed to know what was happening to my body so that I could figure out what to do next.

The instructions on the box said that I needed to wait two minutes, but right away lines started to form on the tests. Two of them. Bold and pink lines that let me know that my body was no longer my own.

I stared at the lines, hearing an odd sort of ringing in my ears as my vision tunneled and all I could focus on was the test. Those lines. Lines that I couldn't tear my eyes away from.

I was pregnant.

My little one was okay. I hadn't lost my pregnancy during the panic attack.

Tears leaked out of the corners of my eyes, pooling there without me being able to do a thing to stop them. Leaking down onto the grubby linoleum floor. I brushed away the wet streaks on my face harshly.

Lightly, I pressed my hand against my stomach and whispered, "I'm sorry, I didn't mean to do it. I promise that I'm going to take care of you."

I thought that I would be panicked at the idea of an unplanned pregnancy. Already, I was socially outcasted from the rest of the Stonevalley wolves. Now I wasn't even sure if I even still would be able to have a relationship with my little one's father. But all I could feel was relief that my stupidity hadn't made me lose my baby.

Yes, I didn't fit in. I might not get any support. But my wolf and I were strong enough to tear apart anyone who wanted to harm this child.

All right, first order of business. I needed to eat something.

I walked back to the snack aisle, counting out the

remaining bills in my pocket. I grabbed the original beef jerky flavor. At least it didn't have jalapeños in it. Probably better for a growing kid, right? I went through the snack aisles, picking options that looked the least unhealthy.

Baby needed to eat after all.

I hesitated as soon as I stepped out of the store, a plastic bag filled with snacks at my side, hand crammed into a bag of beef jerky.

What was I going to do now?

The Edgeriver territory wasn't an option, but the world was a big place. I could make my way down to the city. It wasn't the safest option for a shifter to be on their own as a lone wolf, but it was possible. I could find a job and a place to stay. Far away from all the pack politics. I couldn't face the thought of living in the castle with Aaron and watching him be with someone else.

Within me, my wolf whined at the thought of running from him. Leaving my mate behind without a word, without an explanation. She paced within me, anxious at the very idea of it.

If I left, would the River wolves view my action as a violation of the treaty? Would me leaving be enough to reignite the war between our packs?

If I was being completely honest with myself, one thought nagged at me. More than the thought of violating the treaty and starting a war. More than the temptation of finding a place where I could be accepted. I couldn't leave without letting him know. I was sure that he would want me to tell him about the pregnancy. I wasn't trying to trap him with a baby or make him change his mind about his upcoming marriage. There was no way I wanted to make him feel forced to be in a relationship with me. But even if we were going to go our separate ways, Aaron deserved to know. It was his baby, too. He deserved to know the truth.

I had to tell him.

30

AARON

My blood pressure was rising along with the panic in my body, adrenaline pounding through my veins. Sofia wasn't anywhere. Not in her room. Not in the Great Hall, or the chapel, or any of the common areas. She hadn't gone to any of her classes.

I had to find her.

If I was being perfectly honest with myself, it was obvious that I wasn't able to find any trace of her because she wasn't in the castle at all. Her scent was clearest in her room, before it crossed with Mother's overpowering fragrance of vanilla and clove.

Whatever Mother had said made Sofia vomit all over her bathroom.

White hot anger flooded through me. I bared my teeth, feeling the tips of fangs pierce into my gums. Every one of my muscles felt tense with rage. Ready to erupt into action.

Why the fuck did it have to be my own mother who was trying to fuck up my relationship with my soulmate? With her pitying look, like she was doing it for my own good. Like she alone knew what was best for me. The urge to break something was overwhelming. I couldn't believe that she'd betray me like this.

What had Mother told my soulmate? Had she merely repeated her fantasy that I was going to marry another woman? Had she told her some other outrageous lies? Whatever Mother said was enough to make Sofia leave the castle.

What if something happened to her?

Without warning, I pictured Sofia how I had found her the last time the soulmark burned with echoes of her pain. Just inches from death by the time I had gotten to her. How she had been brutalized. With that bastard pressing the chain into her neck, his face contorted with exertion and traces of excitement. Silver burning into her delicate skin.

No. I couldn't lose her. Not now when plans were coming together. Not now when I'd found a way to get to keep her. I needed her back. I had to fix whatever damage Mother had done to our relationship.

Enough was enough.

I retraced her path from her room, down the stairways to the little used doorway by the stables. The same exit she'd snuck through weeks ago. Where I'd grabbed her bare arm, touching her skin for the first time. The same spot where our soulmarks bloomed to life between us. At the very least, the soulmark wasn't burning now. Whatever had happened, Sofia didn't seem like she had come to any physical harm.

She'd headed out toward the forest and hadn't gotten far before shifting to the wolf. Her scent was partially washed away by light rains.

When my wolf demanded to follow her, I didn't protest. He erupted out. It didn't feel like I was shifting so much as he was breaking through my chest. Bursting through my bones and ripping his way free. All my muscles pulled as my bones snapped into place and reformed. I shifted; the process seemed faster than it had ever been as the beast within me forced his way to the surface.

My wolf ran. Unleashed, my wolf bolted across the forest, tearing across the land like a wildfire. He dismissed the faint trail that revealed Sofia's path. Instead, he ran to the north, cutting across the Stonevalley territory. My wolf showed no hesitation, following instincts I couldn't process. Moving with single-minded determination. Trees blurred past me. Deers, scavengers, other animals dashed to get out of the way. The wolf's pace was absolutely brutal.

I didn't question the wolf's instinct, even as I ran to the furthest reaches of the Stonevalley territory. I caught her scent when she was about a mile out. Frantically analyzing everything over the last distance between us. She didn't seem to be hurt; at least there was no scent of blood on the wind.

When her scent was clearer, my wolf put on an extra burst of speed. Straining and pushing, desperate to get closer to her.

The moment that Sofia spotted me, she stilled. Stopping right in her tracks. Relief flooded my system once I had eyes on her. She was in unfamiliar, worn-down clothes, with a plastic bag at her side. She seemed to be heading back toward the Stonevalley territory rather than leaving it. But my mate was safe. Nothing else mattered as much as that.

My wolf was practically basking in her scent, pressing his nose against her warm skin. Nostrils flared wide, practically inhaling her. There was something different about her scent. A change in her hormones that I hadn't encountered before. I wasn't sure what it was. Whatever it was had my wolf excited. His tail was wagging like a puppy, nose practically glued to her.

Sofia's soft human hands stroked the head of my wolf, fondling against his ears. Tears began to form in the corners of her eyes. She looked away from me, sniffling. Her breath came in sharp little inhales as if she were struggling not to cry.

What the fuck did Mother say to her? What had her feeling this way? What lies did I have to dismantle to break through to her?

The wolf knew enough to realize that there was nothing he could do to help her. He pressed his nose against her, inhaling once more deeply before releasing control. Allowing the human form to take over.

I crouched down as the wolf fur folded back into human skin. As my limbs resized, my bones stretched and cracked. Refigured to walk upright on two feet. As claws dulled into blunt human fingers and my fangs shrank back into my jaw.

As soon as I could walk off the shock of transformation, I crossed the last bit of distance to Sofia and pulled her into an embrace. Sofia stiffened in my hold. Why? Was she angry at me? Was she scared of me again? This wasn't fair; everything between us got all twisted up.

"Are you hurt? What happened?" I pressed my lips against the warmth of her skin. Not quite a kiss. "Please, tell me."

Instead of responding, tears pooled in the corners of her eyes, leaking down like miniature rivers. She was tense, and so nervous she was practically shaking.

I stroked soothing patterns down her back. She was stiff with so much tension it was practically rolling off her in waves.

"Was it something my mother said? Please tell me that you don't believe any of her nonsense. None of it is true." I wanted to pull her tighter against me. I wanted to take her mouth in a claiming kiss, push her down to the forest floor and press into her until she never again questioned how deeply I wanted her. So she'd know without a shadow of a doubt that she belonged to me.

She didn't say anything for a moment, instead leaning against me and taking steadying breaths. She felt so little and so tired.

Her breath shuddered. In a small voice, she finally spoke.

"I found out that I'm pregnant."

I stilled for a moment as my mind went blank.

What?

The vomit I'd found in her room. I'd gotten it wrong.

I didn't know what I was expecting for her to say until I realized that it definitely wasn't that. I pulled away far enough that I could look into her eyes. But Sofia was still refusing to meet my gaze.

Her lips quivered. Sofia spoke faster, as if forcing herself to get the words out. "I found out right before your mother came to my room and basically told me that I can never be anything more than your whore. That you're marrying someone else."

I gripped Sofia by her shoulders, gazing at her steadily even though she wouldn't look back at me. "Hey, that isn't happening. I'm not marrying any other woman. No other woman could ever match the fire in you. No one else could even come close." I couldn't believe that Mother would call Sofia a whore. I didn't even want to repeat it. Didn't want that disgusting accusation to leave my lips. "I can't believe that she'd call you that. It's such bullshit. You are the only woman I want to be with."

Sofia acted like she hadn't even heard me. She just sniffed loudly, shaking her head. "I wasn't thinking. I walked out of the castle and just panicked... My wolf took over."

It was like a switch went off in my brain, flipping from shocked to numb pain.

My chest felt as if it were growing heavy. All the warmth was pulled out of me. Everything went ice-cold.

Shifting was a death sentence for a fetus. It was essentially an abortion.

She hadn't even spoken to me about it.

I tried to remember how hard Sofia's life was. How she had almost no one in her corner. How she had almost all of her choices taken from her. Maybe she didn't want to have a baby. After everything else was taken away from her, I couldn't fault her. It was her body after all.

But at the same time. Fuck.

I didn't have any strong feelings about fatherhood before, but now faced with the thought of it, I realized I could almost picture what our child might look like. What I might want to name them. What it would feel like to see Sofia as a mother. For us to be a family.

I couldn't believe she took that away without at least talking to me first.

Before speaking, I cleared my throat. Careful not to pull away from her or show her any signs of how her words tore into me. Sofia had gone through enough. The last thing I wanted to do was to make this any worse.

It wasn't like Sofia did this on purpose. It sounded like it was a mistake. She'd just panicked.

"It's okay," I lied. It wasn't okay. Not really. But I wasn't about to admit that to her. "It wasn't your fault. We can always try again. Whenever you're ready."

"What?" It was like my words somehow jolted her out

of whatever strained headspace she was in. "What are you talking about?"

"I'm just saying that I understand. My mother lied. I can only imagine how awful that must have felt. I'm sorry that you lost the baby. I wish that I'd been there for you." As I spoke, a dizzying emptiness opened within me. I had to get a grip.

I had to remember that I was holding my soulmate in my arms. I'd found her. She was alive and well. That was the most important thing. That had to be the most important thing. Because what would happen if I had lost her? I had to remember that I came so close to losing her.

Death wanted a piece of my mate.

Members of my pack wanted me with another.

My own fucking mother wanted to take her away from me.

Fuck all of that.

As long as there was any life left within my body, any strength left in my bones, I would fight to keep her. She was my soulmate. Mine.

"I didn't." She swallowed nervously. "I'm still pregnant. I came back to tell you. I felt like I had to at least tell you."

I stared into Sofia's dove-gray eyes as her words slowly sunk into my skull. Piercing through the fog of despair hanging over me. I didn't have any words to say. It was as if light slowly dug through the swell of dark emotions within me. It wasn't too late. I hadn't had my future, my little family, ripped away from me with one violent lie. One miscommunication.

Sofia spoke fast, and the air thickened with the sharp scent of her nervousness. "I don't want you to change any plans that you might have. Or make you feel forced to have to take care of a baby. I just wanted to let you know that I'm pregnant. I just thought that you deserved to know. If that's not what you want, I understand. I can do it on my own. I could always..."

Her voice trailed off as I reached for her, cradling her face in the palm of my hands.

"I love you."

Sofia gasped, staring back at me with wide eyes.

I let one hand drop down to rest over her belly. "I love our baby already."

Sofia's lip quivered as her eyes grew watery.

My gaze was locked on hers. Demanding that she hear me out. That she hear the truth of what I had to say. Each word felt heated by the raw emotion I forced myself to hold back.

"There's nothing I want more than to be there for our child. I'd be honored if you let me be a part of your life. Both of you. However you'll let me. I want to marry you. If you would have me. I want to be with you if you don't. As long as I can keep you in my life. That is all I want."

Sofia was crying again. The tears streamed out freely now. The tension within her finally snapped, and she leaned into me. Letting me hold her.

I could feel her nodding against me. In a voice barely louder than a breath, a voice I wouldn't have been able to hear without the senses of a wolf, Sofia answered me.

"Yes."

I kissed her, tasting the salt on her lips from her tears. Tasting beneath it to the fiery brilliance and utter sweetness of the woman I loved.

31

SOFIA

Aaron insisted on carrying me the rest of the way to the castle—the impossibly stubborn man. Even though he was barefoot, and completely bare. Because he was completely naked.

"I can walk," I muttered sheepishly to him.

"Let me take care of you," he'd whispered back to me. With heat in his eyes and in his voice. Like he was hinting that he wanted to do so much more than carry me.

The warmth in his words made me shiver. So I let him carry me. If I was being perfectly honest, I was tired. Exhausted from running across the entire Stonevalley territory as a wolf. Through a quarter of the Edgeriver territory in human form. I was just emotionally drained from all the revelations of the day.

It was nice. It was so nice to settle against the warmth of Aaron's skin. The solid feel of his chest as he held me. The way his muscles contracted and bunched as he moved. It felt like being held by a pillar of strength.

He carried me all the way over to a supply drop off bin, where he briefly put me down as he threw on some shoes and clothes. As soon as he was dressed, Aaron swept me up into his arms once more, carrying me bridal style.

"Did you mean it?" Aaron murmured the words close to the shell of my ear.

Something in the deep timber of his voice resonated deep within me. His words heated me up inside, flooding my core with warmth. Soothing away all the anxiety I had built up ever since I discovered I was pregnant.

Aaron cared for me. It was clear in the reverent way that he held me, in the way that he looked at me. I couldn't believe how quick I was to dismiss all of that. To assume the absolute worst in him. How could I think that he just wanted to use me? That he would be willing to throw me away?

Aaron told me he *loved* me.

"Mean what?" My voice came out groggy. The gentle rocking motion of his walking gait was lulling me half to sleep.

"Do you want to marry me?"

I blushed so hard I was sure that my skin was red down to my toes.

"Yes." Goddess, yes. I might have buried it down deep, but there was a part of me that always wanted to be married. I didn't think I ever obsessed over the style of the dress, the flowers for the venue or that sort of thing. But I wanted to be married. I had always wanted to find someone that I could spend the rest of my life with. In the bolder days of my youth, I dared dream about what it would feel like to become a wolf. To find my soulmate.

For a long while now, if I pictured someone that I could spend the rest of my life with, the image conjured up in my mind would be of Aaron. I couldn't even imagine being with anyone else.

Aaron swallowed. I was close enough to him to watch the dip and bob of his Adam's apple. "All right, then."

Aaron didn't mention it again. He probably needed time to plan something out. Which was fine. The two of us were shifters—we'd likely have an extended lifespan. We might have hundreds of years to spend together. There wasn't any rush.

I settled back against him, letting him carry me all the way to the castle. I was still pretty drowsy, and I didn't realize that he didn't take me back to my room until a rough voice, dripping with authority, called out.

"Took you long enough."

I stiffened in Aaron's hold, rising up to get a look at my surroundings.

We were in a room I had never entered before, but by the quality of the furnishings—velvet drapery, crown molding, crystal chandelier—I could tell that this was one of the rooms of the noble families. It wasn't until my eyes flicked to the heavy oak table that I noticed the alpha seated there.

The alpha was undeniably dominant. Power seeped from his pores. From his broad wingspan and the cruel curve of sleek muscles. Blue eyes that were paler than Aaron's pierced me. Ice-like and perceptive. He had a gaze sharp enough to cut through my skull and examine the thoughts swirling around my mind. Capable of seeing straight through me and assessing my exact worth.

Holding my gaze, the alpha nodded at me—and with that simple gesture I felt acceptance wash over me.

Though his features were handsome, there was an edge to them. Like time itself had filed away at them. Though the alpha looked similar to his son, his presence was sharper.

My back straightened. I was tense all over as if I had been caught doing something wrong. Custom dictated that I should be curtsying, not lounging in Aaron's arms like an invalid.

The alpha snorted at the sight of me tripping over myself. "Are you ready for a wedding or a nap?"

My gaze flicked over to Aaron, as if I could ask him with my expression: wait, *now?*

He smiled back at me sheepishly in reply. Striding to the oak desk, he placed me on my feet.

"Hold each other's hands," the alpha directed.

I laid my hands into Aaron's much bigger palms.

Was this happening? This didn't feel real.

Only a few hours ago I was seriously considering running away to the city. Starting my life completely over with the small handful of bills in my pocket and the borrowed shirt on my back. Now I was marrying the heir to the alpha?

But looking at Aaron, any fears that might have risen to the surface were stomped out by the fierce triumph of his expression. Certainty sunk all the way down deep within me that this was right.

"To each of you, there shall be one bond. To bind blood in blood. To bind bone in bone. Twin souls, blessed by the goddess, and forged in the pale moon's glow. For no mortal hindrance to tear asunder."

At the words of the alpha, I felt jolts of electricity flicker from the point where my hands held his in a warm energy that pulsed all the way up my limbs, settling deep within me.

"As alpha, I grant you, Aaron Ragnolf, and you, Sofia Ragnolf, with the bond of marriage. Do you accept?"

"Yes." Aaron's voice rang out immediately and clear.

"Yes." My own voice was smaller and almost breathless.

Once the affirmation slipped out of my lips, my soul-mark pulsed in a moment of bright heat.

"Then as alpha, I shall bestow upon you these blessings. May you join in body as you are already joined in soul. May love embrace you. May the goddess keep you. May your union never fall to loneliness. May even death fail to part you."

I felt the authority of the alpha's words sink through my skin. Coursing through my body and growing each and every one of the ties between us. Strengthening our connection in unbreakable bonds—bonds forged in something feral and wild that connected his soul to mine.

Until nothing could deny the truth of it. We were married.

32

AARON

Sofia slept like a tree stump. A warm tree stump. She was so comfortable that it was hard to leave her in the morning. Though I wanted to kiss her and greet her with sweet nothings, the last thing I wanted was to wake her. She was worn out.

The least I could do after our rushed marriage was give her the proper honeymoon experience. I'd fucked her five times last night.

Sofia was my *wife*.

She was fierce and lovely. Everything that I needed and had no idea I even wanted in a woman.

Pregnant with my child.

A warmth bloomed throughout my stomach at the thought of it. I wanted to lay in bed with her until she woke and have a repeat of last night.

But duty called.

My desk held a veritable mountain of paperwork. The work had seemed to multiply, as I had abandoned it for most of the day and ended up running for miles searching for Sofia.

As soon as I became the alpha, I was going to delegate a good chunk of these menial tasks to someone else. I had more important things to do. Like my woman.

A sharp rap on the outside of my office jolted me out of my thoughts. Mother didn't even wait for me to respond before she opened the door, stepping inside my workspace.

"Aaron, the alpha is summoning you."

Her perfume wasn't enough to mask her emotions. The rabid arrogance came across loud and clear from the subtle smirk on her face.

Was this it, then? Was she making her move? Mother was moving faster than I had anticipated.

It was a good thing that I had moved faster.

I forced myself not to look away from her, though I wanted to tear my gaze away. I didn't want to look at the smug expression on her face.

I followed Mother through the hallways to the alpha's quarters. It wasn't surprising at all to find Tora and her parents already seated at the oak table, and the alpha with a dazed expression on his face.

It seemed that Mother was moving her chess pieces across the board. Well, we would see how effective she could be at convincing me to commit bigamy.

I nodded deferentially to the alpha. "You asked to see me."

The resentment I'd felt toward him had faded. He was a sick man, but that didn't change who he was. He might have been trapped within his own failing mind, unable to live by his truths, but none of that was his choice. Clearly, on one of his good days, he'd chosen to help me.

It wasn't hard to tell that the alpha was having one of his bad days today.

He seemed jittery. The scent of his agitation was clouding the room with the acidic chemical stench of cortisol.

He didn't meet my eyes, and instead arranged and rearranged the pens on his desk.

"Your father called you here to discuss your upcoming wedding," Mother spoke for him.

I didn't look at Tora and her parents. Didn't acknowledge them.

They might not have any blame for this farce of a marriage alliance. I didn't know how much they knew. How much of what they had been told was truth, and how much was the truth stretched into something unrecognizable. The Hansens could have been innocent in all of this. I had no problems with Tora. She was fine. A good soldier. A valuable member of the pack. It wasn't her fault how completely she paled in comparison to Sofia.

But I had no interest in paying any mind to Mother's games any longer.

I decided that it was time to cut through the bullshit.

"Do you know who I am?" I was genuinely curious. Was he able to recognize me today?

"Don't be ridiculous. You're my son and heir."

"What's my name?" I held his gaze patiently.

The alpha scoffed. "You are my eldest. Erik."

I heard scratches from across the room, sounding distinctly like Mother digging her claws into the alpha's antique table.

"So, to be clear, you are planning on arranging a marriage between Erik Decoteau and this woman?"

"Aaron!" Mother yelled out sharply, as if I were nothing more than a disobedient child. "This is completely disrespectful to the Hansens. Enough is enough. You have a duty to fulfill to your pack. We can no longer afford to let you shirk your responsibilities."

"What responsibilities do you mean?" I drummed my fingertips against the table, completely at ease. Mother wouldn't be able to carry out any of her threats. Without the teeth behind her demands, she just looked ridiculous.

"You have a duty to marry responsibly. To continue the bloodline and provide the pack with future generations."

"My wife is already pregnant."

I said the words blandly. Enjoying the confusion on Mother's face as she processed what I had said. Replaced with the look of complete shock that she wasn't able to hide.

The room went silent. The only sound was the gentle click of pens as they were rearranged on the desk.

Mother had been bold, but even she wasn't bold enough to demand that I divorce my pregnant wife. At least not in front of a prospective bride. In front of a father demonstrating unmistakable problems with his memory. This meeting was just the perfect amount of chaos to throw all her schemes out the window.

Mother glared at me with wide eyes. In a moment, she might recover and demand an explanation. But I didn't think that either Sofia or I owed her anything.

I stood casually. Careful to keep a vengeful smile off my face.

"I don't think I'm needed here. Good luck arranging your nuptials with Erik."

I hadn't expected Sofia's attendance at dinner tonight. Typically, she only attended the formal dinners once a week or even biweekly. I couldn't blame her. If I was able to get away with it, I would want to get out of the public eye occasionally.

She stood at the dining hall entrance wearing a gorgeous white dress, all in fine satin. It hinted at her curves, at her perfect hourglass figure. The long slit up the slide revealed shapely legs underneath.

Gorgeous.

It would have been the perfect dress to wear for a wedding ceremony.

The inside of my mouth went dry—was she wearing it for me? Watching her walk toward me at the dining hall was like watching her walk down an aisle at a formal wedding. Like she was giving me the experience we hadn't been able to have.

I briefly worried about having to watch her sit at another table. I could only imagine the utter frustration of having to watch her from across the dining hall as other men caught glimpses of her perfect body. Instead, Sofia strode across the hall, coming directly toward me.

I typically had a chair or two open next to me, as it was presumptuous to choose seating next to a high-level wolf. Unless invited.

Sofia approached me directly, stopping right in front of my chair. Looking me straight in the eyes, she pulled off one of her long white gloves. Exposing her soulmark in front of everyone in the entire castle.

I knew exactly what she was offering me.

This was a risk for her. If I ignored her gesture, she could effectively become a social outcast. Even worse than what she was already experiencing now. She was offering me a chance to make our relationship public. Leaving herself completely vulnerable.

She trusted me.

I got to my feet, tugging off my glove as well. Revealing the soulmark that I had kept carefully covered for all this time.

I slid my hand up her arm, stopping at the swirls and concentric curves of her soulmark. Lining it up with mine until the patterns and swirls matched up exactly—a perfect pair.

As our marks aligned, they resonated. A flash of light flickered from within the center of each of our marks, surging outward—lighting up and traveling out across the entire pattern written into our skin.

An audible gasp echoed across the entire dining hall.

Without looking, I could tell that all eyes would be on the two of us. But I couldn't take my own eyes away from Sofia's. I would have accepted a secret marriage if that was what she wanted. As long as she was safe, I was willing to limit our relationship to meeting together in the dark. But I couldn't deny that I'd been hoping for exactly this: the chance to make it clear to everyone that Sofia was *mine*.

I knew that Sofia hadn't done this for the status. A public relationship with me might elevate her standings in the pack, but knowing Sofia, that wasn't reason enough to lose her anonymity. Anyone publicly connected to me would be under intense scrutiny, and that was the absolute last thing that she wanted. There was only one reason why she would deliberately give up her secrets. Why she would out herself as a wolf.

She had done it all for me.

Mother was likely furious. This was the moment that

she had been fighting against—the moment that I publicly accepted Sofia as my mate.

Well, then. Now that I had everyone's attention, I'd better give Mother something to really get angry about.

I pulled Sofia close, claiming her lips in a burning kiss.

EPILOGUE

SOFIA
Seven months later

My wolf waited restlessly within me.

It had been so long since I'd shifted into a wolf. If I hadn't been able to sense her feral presence within me, I would swear that I wasn't a shifter at all anymore. Luckily she was patient. I'd heard about women that had to fight a battle of wills with impatient wolves. Horror stories of women who ended up miscarrying at the last moment because of it.

At the thought, my wolf huffed. As if she would ever put the little one in danger like that. My wolf was waiting with stoic patience, as protective of this child as me.

Well, lately I felt like if I was going to shift into anything it would be a walrus. For the first few months of my pregnancy, my belly remained fairly tight. Now I was about the size of a house. I couldn't see my toes for over a month. Putting on shoes and bending down to pick up objects were tasks that were getting beyond me.

Aaron was absolutely ridiculous as my pregnancy progressed. He snarled at anyone who came within feet of me. As if anyone in the castle would dare put a finger on me, the way this beast of an alpha lingered near. I swear that the man was going to give his guards heart attacks.

He had a sofa set up in his office and insisted that I stay there with him as he worked. I was sitting on the sofa now, failing at knitting a baby blanket. For every row I completed, I would find that I dropped a stitch somewhere and needed to go through the rows and figure out where it was all unraveling. I had come very close to unleashing my claws on this fluffy monstrosity. This was supposed to be a relaxing activity.

I was so engrossed at mentally cursing at my yarn that I didn't notice my soulmate joined me on the sofa until I could feel the warmth of his arms as they wrapped around my shoulders. No matter how many times he held me, I couldn't help luxuriating in his touch. It felt like being held by pure strength. Absolutely decadent.

Aaron pressed sinfully hot kisses against my neck. Like he couldn't get enough. He was insatiable. Being kissed by him was being kissed by a raw and primal need. A force of nature.

This man was absolutely everything that I wanted. Even before I knew myself enough to write myself a list of qualities, the moon goddess delivered all of them in one fine muscular package. A shiver went down the entire length of my spine as his large hands gently caressed me.

He whispered into my ear, as he gently stroked my very round, very firm stomach. "There is nothing sexier than seeing your belly swelling with my child."

How did he always know exactly what to say to ignite a fire within me?

I turned his way, putting the knitting project firmly down. I watched the heat in his gaze and was ready to match it with the passion threatening to burn me down. A heat that coursed through my body, settling into my core... and plopped down onto the silk sofa cushions beneath me.

"Oh!" I cried out in an embarrassingly high pitched voice.

"Shit, did I hurt you?" Aaron backed away just far enough to look me over, trying to find the source of my pain.

Oh, no.

What I thought was just normal wetness from his attention, was anything but normal.

Please don't tell me that I had peed myself. I might just die of shame.

"No." I replied, wanting to melt into the floor.

Aaron looked at the liquid on the sofa cushions and his face went pale.

"Did your water just break?"

Oh. Oh, shit.

It wasn't pee. I hadn't made a fool of myself.

The baby was coming.

AARON

THE MOMENT THAT THE PACK DOCTOR PICKED UP MY child, placing the little one on my mate's chest, I felt like my entire world became untethered. All the strings tying me to my family, to my pack. All of them were cut and rearranged, with my small family at the center.

Little milky blue eyes, tentatively opened. Observing the world for the first time.

Our baby was perfect.

I leaned closer to Sofia, who was still panting, trying to catch her breath. "You're amazing." I took a closer look at the tiny form. "We have a son."

Sofia brightened at the sight of him. Seemingly shaking off the fatigue of her fourteen hour labor to get a better look at him.

"He looks like you." She delicately brushed one shaky finger against his tightly curled fist.

"Shame. I wish that he'd look a bit more like his lovely mother. He's got your hair though." Our baby had a few dark tufts of hair at the top of his head. Otherwise, Sofia was right. His little face strongly resembled the shape of my nose and chin.

It was wild. This helpless little person who looked so much like me. A person that we helped bring together into the world.

"What should we name him?"

"We could always name him after my great grandfather, Ragnvald. He was a strong alpha, with a strong name."

"Ragnvald?"

"Yeah."

"Absolutely not."

"Got it."

It was traditional to name potential heirs to the alpha line after strong leaders in the past. I would happily turn my back on tradition if it tried to get between me and my soulmate. Still, an established name would help tie our son to the legacy of the pack. It would help connect him to our history and force the others to recognize him.

I ran through names of past alphas, running down the mental list until I came across a name that I thought was the least offensive.

"What about Leo?"

"Leo." Sophia tried out the name. I immediately loved the way that the name flowed. The sound of it felt right coming out of her lips. "I like it."

Leo.

Watching the small form of my son, I made him a silent vow. Not only to protect him, but to stand against anyone who sought to belittle my flesh and blood for who he is. For who his mother is.

Mother had been getting more persistent over the last few months. When it had become clear to her that I would not be making my customary stops for tea, she had started getting more creative.

She had resorted to adding to my paperwork, by sending written requests for tea. Mailing me letters attempting to apologize to me. Trying to smooth out the tricky business where she tried to force me to marry someone else. As the pregnancy progressed she had gotten more aggressive with her attempts at communication. Asking for more information about the baby.

Once she even had the audacity to ask if I was sure that the child was mine. As if it wasn't obvious that every luscious inch of my mate's body belonged to me. She was mine. No one else would ever touch her.

I made it clear to her that I was not the one that needed an apology, and that I wasn't going to speak another word to her until she could show the proper respect owed to my mate.

The alpha's illness seemed to have broken something within Mother. Yet that was no excuse for the cruelty that she had consistently shown to my wife.

There would always be people who would try to look down on my son and my wife because of their bloodline. Who would consider them unworthy, all because of a multi-generational war. A war that should have run its course long ago.

I would stand against anyone who would deny me the right to love those who I chose to love.

For as long as I had the strength in my body, I would fight for them.

THE END

ABOUT THE AUTHOR

After years of writing, Miyo decided to unleash her wolfish fantasies upon the world.

Shifters. Dominant Alphas. Sweet love and dark fantasy. Miyo is writing this for every reader who wants their characters bent over chairs and called a good girl. For everyone who wants to forget their day-jobs and responsibilities and curl up to read something spicy. For everyone who wants to unlock a world that's just a little bit wild.